Praise for
Death of a Mill Girl

"Richly realized setting and period details, impeccable plotting, and a wise hero made more appealing by his foibles . . . *Death of a Mill Girl* kept me reading straight through and left me eager for Linsley's next."
—Ann McMillan, author of *Dead March*

"Captures the atmosphere of a small, early nineteenth century New England town . . . a pleasant evening's reading."
—*I Love a Mystery*

"The book's strength is . . . in the depiction of farm and mill life in mid-nineteenth century New England . . . vividly described."
—*The Mystery Reader*

"Linsley does not fall into the trap that many other authors of historical fictions fall into; namely, the need to give a history lesson during the course of his prose. Often, writers of this kind of fiction do a politically correct revisionism as well, and Linsley avoids this. [He] does a great job of showing the ugliness and stupidity of prejudice . . . by not clobbering the reader with a brick. He simply shows it in its stark ugliness as a way of life, and allows the reader to draw his/her own conclusions . . . Beede himself is the greatest strength of this novel . . . I hope this becomes a series."
—*Reviewing the Evidence*

SAVING LOUISA

Clyde Linsley

BERKLEY PRIME CRIME, NEW YORK

To Dad and Mother, gratefully

This is a work of fiction. Names, characters, places, and incidents either are the product of the author's imagination or are used fictitiously, and any resemblance to actual persons, living or dead, business establishments, events, or locales is entirely coincidental.

SAVING LOUISA

A Berkley Prime Crime Book / published by arrangement with the author

PRINTING HISTORY
Berkley Prime Crime mass-market edition / November 2003

Copyright© 2003 by Clyde Linsley.
Cover art by Craig Nelson.
Cover design by Rita Frangie.
Text design by Julie Rogers.

ISBN: 0-425-19309-8

Berkley Prime Crime Books are published by
The Berkley Publishing Group,
a division of Penguin Group (USA) Inc.,
375 Hudson Street, New York, New York 10014.
The name BERKLEY PRIME CRIME and the BERKLEY PRIME CRIME design are trademarks belonging to Penguin Group (USA) Inc.

PRINTED IN THE UNITED STATES OF AMERICA

10 9 8 7 6 5 4 3 2 1

Chapter 1

She awoke with the full moon high above the eastern horizon, and she was immediately consumed with shame and fear.

She had not intended to sleep, but he had come to her again, and afterward she had slipped unwillingly into a postcoital drowsiness. She had not resisted him, for she knew that it would be fruitless; he would have his way. Whatever privileges she might have acquired through her service to her mistress, he was a white man, and she was a slave. End of argument.

And so she had given in to him, grudgingly at first, and then less so. It was becoming easier to give in with every passing night: one more reason, out of so many others, why she must leave, and leave quickly.

There were, of course, even more pressing reasons why flight was necessary. She had missed at least one period of bleeding now. She knew what that meant, in all likelihood, and she knew that in a few months she would begin to show, no matter how diligently she attempted to disguise it. If she remained here, her condition would become apparent to all, even her mistress. Nothing good could come of that.

The moon was full and high in the sky, casting a ghostly glow over the fields of stripped, brown cotton stalks. The slave patrols would no doubt be abroad on the main roads, and they would be aided by the glow of the full moon. If she were caught . . .

Perhaps she should wait until the moon entered another quarter, when it would be less brilliant. Perhaps it would be overcast some night soon, and escape would be easier. But she knew that she would go, and go that night. If she waited, her nerve might fail her altogether. It was now or never.

And what if they were to catch her? What could they do to her that was worse than this? Whip her? But she had been whipped before, by her new mistress as by the mistress who preceded her, and had survived.

She dressed quickly and extracted from her straw mat the food she had hidden during the days of planning. It had been nibbled on by mice—or rats—but she could not afford to be squeamish when so much was at stake. She wrapped the food securely in her head scarf and slipped as quietly as she could out the door of the summer kitchen where she slept.

Now or never, she thought to herself. Now or never.

The road was wide and straight. She was alone. She marveled at her good fortune, for she had envisioned a road filled with patty rollers on horseback, armed with shotguns and accompanied by dogs.

But so far there was only the road, vacant and silent, and she was alone. She strode warily ahead, although she knew the empty road might fill up at any moment. The slaver catchers might appear suddenly, ruthless and without warning.

Would they be hiding in the woods beside the road? She glanced fearfully in that direction, but she thought it unlikely. Probably they would come riding down the middle of the road, noisily and without stealth, depending on their dogs to alert them to the presence of runaways.

The woods closed in on either side of the road. If the patrols appeared, she would have to slip quietly into the woods and hope that she had not been seen. Some runaways might have avoided the road altogether, relying on the security of the trees and underbrush, but she was unaccustomed to wilderness and needed the clear pathway that the road provided. There were snakes, too, in the woods.

As she had anticipated, she heard the hounds long before she saw them. The baying came from somewhere ahead of her, and it was growing rapidly louder. For a moment she stood frozen in place. Panic swept over her, and she feared that her escape had ended before it had scarcely begun.

The sound of running feet reached her ears, and a thin, dark figure appeared on the horizon. It came on rapidly, and she heard a young male voice shouting at her.

"They're coming! Hide fast!"

She dove into the underbrush and made herself as invisible as she could, though she feared that it would make no difference. If the dogs did not see her, they might nevertheless *smell* her.

The young man reached the place where she had been standing and passed by without slowing his pace. He had almost made it around the bend in the road when the dogs appeared and set up a tumultuous cacophony of howls.

"There he is!" a voice shouted, and she heard the hoofbeats galloping toward her. The young man left the road and plunged into the woods on the opposite side. The dogs followed an instant later.

The howling grew louder as they closed in on their quarry. She could not see the end of the chase from her hiding place, but neither did she dare to move. Men remained in the road, still on horseback, and might well hear her if she attempted to escape.

The dogs, fortunately, were preoccupied with the young man. Either they had not picked up her scent or they had discounted it as irrelevant to their current quest.

The noise in the underbrush grew louder and nearer. Two of the men dismounted and followed their dogs into the woods where she could not see. They emerged moments later, dragging their quarry by his arms. The young man continued to struggle until one of the mounted men tossed two lengths of heavy rope to the two on the ground. They tied the young man's wrists behind his back and slipped a noose around his neck. Then, pulling him roughly along behind them, they turned and started back the way they had come. The young man was forced to run in order to avoid strangulation.

No words had been spoken since the slave catchers

had pursued their victim into the underbrush. Now even the baying of the hounds and the clatter of horses' hooves subsided.

She should take advantage of this respite to move on. Her absence had escaped notice so far, but it was only a matter of time before she would be missed. But first she would rest to allow her heart to slow down and the shiver of fear to pass.

"**M**iz Hawkins!"

The sheriff pounded the door with the flat of his hand. The sound echoed through the dark house, followed by silence.

"See what I mean, Sheriff? She's usually a light sleeper. This ain't like her."

The sheriff looked around the upstairs landing as if an answer to the mystery might be lurking there before returning his gaze to his deputy standing beside him.

"You sure she ain't gone visiting somebody?"

"She don't hardly leave the house no more. She don't get around so good these days."

The sheriff turned back to banging on the door.

"Miz Hawkins! It's Sheriff Schneider! You all right in there?"

Still no answer. The sheriff turned to his deputy. "All right, Howie, have your boys break it down.

Two attempts were enough. The pine boards splintered and gave way, and they were inside.

"My God," someone said.

The old woman lay on her back on the narrow bed. A round, red hole had opened her breast an inch or so from her heart. Her eyes stared at the ceiling, and at the flies that were already congregating.

"Should we get the doc?" Howie said.

"There ain't no chance she's alive," Sheriff Schneider said. "But yeah, get the doctor. He can dig out the ball, at least. Maybe that'll tell us something."

"But I'm damned if I know what," he said to himself when Howie had left.

Chapter 2

"The river gets real twisty up here," the pilot said as he pointed the little merchantman a notch into the wind. "Sometimes you can see ships backed up here for miles, waiting for the wind to change."

"I know," Josiah Beede said, although he was aware that the pilot, intent on his change in tack, did not hear him.

"They call this section English Turn," the pilot said. "Never did know why."

"It's a long story."

"Well," said the pilot, "I ain't got time for long stories just now. If it's a Frog story, it probably ain't that interesting, anyways."

Beede moved to the rail and peered through the afternoon sunlight. Around this bend, or perhaps the next, would be the place he had been awaiting with in-

creasing eagerness for nearly an hour. He had forgotten
how long the trip could take from the mouth of the great
river to the battlefield that had taken his brother from
him and the city that had given him—however
briefly—a wife and child.

If by some miracle the river could be straightened
out, the trip would take very little time. As it was, the
distance from the gulf to New Orleans was well over a
hundred miles of meanders, switchbacks, sandbars, tree
trunks, and other debris that had been ripped by the
river and its tributaries from the soil of half a continent.
In consequence, the journey was long and tiring as the
ship, tacking constantly, muscled its way against the
wind and current.

"How's your nigger doin'?" the pilot asked as the
ship swung onto its new tack. "I saw him up on deck
when I came aboard. That the way you treat your slaves
up north? Give 'em the run of the ship?"

"We don't have slaves up north," Beede said. "He's
my companion, and he's a free man."

"Free man, huh? That's a waste of a good nigger, if
you ask me. Well, he'd better watch hisself when he
crosses the street or he won't be a free man much
longer. They need strong backs in the cotton fields upriver. Sugar plantations downstream, too."

"He has his papers. They won't bother him in New
Orleans."

The pilot took his eye off the wheel to look at Beede.

"Been here before, huh?"

"I lived here once."

"Been a little while, though, I'd wager," the pilot
said. "Things have changed. It's an American city
now."

"Is it so very different?" Beede asked.

"Depends on who you ask, I guess," the pilot said with a shrug. "One thing that's changed, though—we don't coddle our niggers the way them Frenchies do."

Beede thought of Randolph, his neighbor and his former slave, who had chosen to remain belowdecks once the ship had entered the mouth of the Mississippi. Despite his manumission, Beede realized, Randolph recognized the danger of his situation.

Beede took his leave of the pilot and went below. He found Randolph as he had left him an hour before, sitting on the edge of his bunk, staring straight ahead at the ship's timbers, as if mesmerized. Close by his side was the small cotton drawstring bag in which Randolph kept dried cranberries. From time to time he would reach absently into the bag and pop another morsel in his mouth. Randolph had discovered cranberries not long after he had moved to New England, and they seemed to have won his heart and soul.

"Are you well?" Beede asked. He knew what this journey was costing his companion, returning to the place where he had been enslaved for so many years. How could it not affect him?

Randolph stirred.

"I have been thinking," he said. "What shall I sow, when spring comes again? How much wheat? How much corn? Which fields should lie fallow? It is all new to me, and these matters occupy my mind constantly."

"No thoughts of your wife?"

"I try not to think of her," Randolph said. "I have not received a letter from her in more than a year, before she was sold down the river. Whenever I think of what this may mean, I am filled with dread."

"We shall know soon enough," Beede said. "Come up on deck with me. We'll be landing shortly."

Randolph shook his head. "I'll stay below."

"Do you have no interest in seeing how New Orleans may have changed in our absence?"

"This city holds no allure for me."

Beede returned to the deck. The ship rounded English Turn, and the city appeared ahead of him on the right-hand bank. At first he saw only the tip of the cathedral steeple above the levee; then, as they approached closer, the building itself, and the Place D'Armes became visible. And farther on, the docks. The waterfront was busier than he had ever seen it, busier, indeed, than he could ever have imagined. Steamboats and sailing vessels filled the river almost to overflowing, and the docks swarmed with people. Slaves, visitors, sailing crews, cotton factors, and sugar merchants milled and shouted. Handcarts and mule-drawn wagons shouldered their way through the crowds, hardly pausing to give stragglers the time to move out of their paths. Atop the levee, a knot of men and women stood amid stacks of trunks and carpetbags, no doubt intending to board one of the paddlewheel packet boats that steamed impatiently in midriver, awaiting the opportunity to move to shore.

Beede stood at the deck rail and watched in astonishment. This was not the New Orleans he had known.

"Amazing!" he said aloud.

"What's that?"

"The port! I've never seen it so busy!"

The pilot shrugged. "This is only half of it," he said. "Look upstream to the other side of the crescent. It's just as busy up there."

"How long has it been like this?"

"Don't know. Ain't been here all that long, myself. Came about five years ago. It was pretty busy then, too."

"Is this as bad as it gets?"

"Pretty much," the pilot said. "A little worse when the cotton crop comes in, I guess. Wasn't it like this when you lived here?"

"No. Not at all."

"You gotta remember," the pilot said. "Like I told you before. This ain't no two-bit French trading post anymore. This is a real city, now. An *American* city."

Beede went below once more to fetch Randolph as the ship hove to and was towed to the quayside. They disembarked into a shouting, jostling mob. From the corner of his eye, Beede could see Randolph's grim face and imagined he could hear the darker man's teeth grinding as they pressed their way through the teeming mass. He understood the man's apprehension, for he, too, felt overwhelmed by the crowd, which seemed both busier and angrier than there was any need for.

They were almost to the levee when Randolph stumbled forward, falling against a large man, in a bedraggled top hat, who whipped around in barely contained fury. Grabbing Randolph by the shoulder, he raised his cane in preparation for striking.

"Goddamn nigger! You watch where you're going!" The man lowered the cane and whipped it across Randolph's back instead of his head. Randolph dropped to the ground with a grimace of pain but without making a sound.

The man raised his cane again and brought it down on Randolph's back once more. A third time he raised his cane, but he did not strike, for Beede grasped the cane with both hands and prevented it.

The man turned on Beede. "Release my cane, sir! I am teaching this boy a lesson, and you are interfering!"

"I am saving you from a thrashing," Beede said. "This *man* is strong enough to snap you like a twig. You should thank me for sparing you many days of agony."

The man bristled. "I'd like to see him try," he said. "Clearly you're unaware of the penalty for a slave who strikes a white man. I hear the flat tones of a Yankee in your voice, sir, but you're not in the North now. You are in my country, and we do not suffer insolence from servants."

"I lived in New Orleans for many years," Beede said as calmly as he could manage. "I know the way of things here. Moreover, this man is not a slave, but a free man—a free man who has been tempered by years of hard farming in rocky soil. You would be well advised to leave him alone before you bite off more than you are able to chew."

"We'll see about that."

A crowd was gathering, and Beede realized that its sympathies were not necessarily aligned with his. Scanning the faces that surrounded him, he saw that they were, in the main, curious rather than aggravated. But they were mostly white faces, from whom little consideration could be expected. He realized that he had placed Randolph in great danger—and perhaps himself as well—if he continued to take Randolph's part.

Well, he thought, it can't be helped. He stepped back from the man and assumed what he imagined to be a fighting stance. From the corner of his eye he saw Randolph move subtly to the side. He had no doubt that the two of them could handle the man between them unless he received assistance from the crowd.

Top Hat seemed to sense this as well, for his glance moved rapidly, and nervously, from one to the other. He clutched the cane so tightly that his knuckles were white, and he ran his tongue uneasily around his lips.

"The colored man was pushed!"

The voice came from behind him. A white man, immaculate in frock coat and stovepipe hat, stepped between Beede and his antagonist. He addressed himself to the man with the cane.

"He was pushed from behind, sir. He meant no offense. I saw the affair in its entirety, and I assure you that he is without blame."

"You're certain of this?"

"Absolutely. A stevedore brushed against him as he passed, causing the boy to stumble. It could not have been prevented."

Beede saw a flicker of relief in the eyes of his antagonist.

"Very well, then," the man with the cane said. "I am content."

He turned to Beede. "Please accept my apologies, sir. If I came to an inaccurate conclusion, I am terribly sorry."

He extended his hand. Beede ignored it. "Your apology would be more properly offered to my friend. He is the one whom you beat with your cane."

The man flushed with anger. "Do not tempt fate," he said. "As a Yankee you cannot be my equal, or I would call you out on this spot. I do not apologize to niggers."

He turned on his heel and stormed away. The crowd, deprived of its spectacle, broke up and moved off.

Beede let a sigh of relief escape his lips. It had been a near thing, and he was unequipped for a duel. After all those years in New Orleans as a young man, doing what was necessary to avoid affairs of honor, he had barely escaped a challenge within an hour of his return. It did not bode well.

"Thank you for your assistance, sir," Randolph said. "I could not have defended myself in the presence of so many people. Even if I had been successful, the crowd would have retaliated against me. At the very least I would have been badly hurt. At worst, I would have been killed."

"I know," Beede said. "I had forgotten what it was like. If not for the gentleman who intervened on our behalf, we might both have been killed by the mob."

He looked around for their defender, but he had vanished into the departing crowd.

"I meant to thank him," Beede said.

"Perhaps we can both thank him on the *next* occasion," Randolph said. "That assumes, of course, that he is nearby and willing to intervene on the next occasion."

"I hadn't thought things through before I spoke," Beede admitted. "I apologize for putting you in danger."

"I was in danger the moment our ship left Baltimore," Randolph said. "And I shall continue to be in danger until we return. If I were less determined to find Louisa, I should never have come back."

"Well, we are here, now," Beede said. "And I am determined to find your wife, if she can be found. We need an ally, however: a guide who can be our eyes and ears in the slave market."

There was one such man, and they both knew him.

• • •

The house they were seeking stood on Rue Royale, near Esplanade. Like its neighbors on either side, it was built of a soft, rose-colored native brick, which peeked out in spots from behind the yellowing stucco covering that had been plastered over the brick for protection against the sun and rain. The street-level floor was given over to a shop, this one devoted to the sale of wine. The louvered shutters were a deep green, and the Spanish-style fan light windows above the door of the house gave it an inviting appearance.

At the door, Randolph lingered behind, and when Beede turned to ask if something was amiss, his friend shook his head.

"I think it best that you go alone," he said. "He will not be pleased to see me, nor will I be pleased to see him."

"Surely you're mistaken. He was a good friend."

"No," Randolph said. "He was *your* friend. He was my *owner*. The two relationships are quite different."

"Please, stay with me. I have hopes that he might offer us the hospitality of his house."

"I don't want it," Randolph said. "And in any event, he will not offer any hospitality to me. If I am with you, he may not offer it to you, either."

"But where will you stay?"

"I have friends," Randolph said. "I know people here. You needn't concern yourself with me. Learn what you can, then seek me in the morning at Congo Square. Someone there will know where to find me."

"Nonsense," Beede said, and turned to knock on the door. But when he turned back, Randolph had already vanished into the crowd.

•   •   •

The door was answered by a young girl with a café au lait complexion, who listened to Beede's prologue in silence and scampered away, leaving him standing at the threshold. A few minutes passed, and he thought that he had, perhaps, been forgotten. But after a while she returned, dropped a quick curtsy, and bade him enter, still without speaking. He waited in the front room amid the wine bottles.

"Josiah! It's so good to see you again."

Pierre Dumond looked old. He had been a youthful forty when Beede had seen him last. He was barely sixty-three, even now, but the intervening years had not been kind. In 1815 he had stood nearly as tall as Andrew Jackson; now he was bowed and frail-looking, with skin the consistency of paper. He had gone everywhere with a cane when Beede had known him before, but it had been merely an embellishment, an accessory he employed mostly for appearances. Now, it was clear, he depended on it, as if it alone kept him vertical.

"It's good to see you, too, Pierre," Beede said, taking the man's hand. "I confess I was not certain that I would be welcome here."

"You need have no fear, Josiah," the old man said. "What's past is past. You were good for Adrienne, and I do not begrudge you my daughter."

"Would that I had kept her better."

"Ah," Dumond said, "I know your feeling. But I also know you loved her more than any other man could have done. If she *could* have been saved, I doubt not that you would have found a way to do so."

"I daresay Madame Dumond would not feel as you do," Beede said.

The old man nodded. "You are probably correct. Unfortunately, Margarethe is no longer with us. She passed away a few years ago in one of our summer pestilences. The yellow fever."

"I am sorry for your loss." I should have kept in touch, he thought. Then I wouldn't have to learn of her matters so late.

"As am I," Dumond said. "Now I am alone, aside from my household servants. It is a lonely life, I fear. If it were not for my business, I would be sick at heart."

"Your shop prospers?"

"Indeed it does. But then, New Orleans has always been good for the wine business. I am even developing a small clientele among the Americans, although I fear they will ever be partial to whiskey and rum."

"The city appears to be overrun with Americans."

"That is also true," Dumond said. "And they are a mixed blessing, at best. There can be no doubt that they have invigorated the city. We are now the fifth-largest city in the nation, and the largest, by far, in the southern states. Trade has never been more brisk, despite the recent bank panic. Fortunes are won and lost daily. More won than lost, I should say."

"But on the other hand?"

"Yes, on the other hand. On the other hand, the old ways are disappearing. The Americans have robbed our lives of many of their pleasures in their relentless pursuit of commercial advantage. They have changed the Carnival season from a celebration of love and life into a coarse, raucous series of drunken brawls."

"We are a young nation, still," Beede said defensively. "We are growing quickly, taking on territory at a breathtaking pace, but we are, in the main, still inhabitants of the wilderness."

Dumond gestured impatiently. "I know that, Josiah. When your vast territories are more settled, I daresay, your people will become more civilized. And not all Americans are ruffians or buffoons, even now. Your General Jackson is a rough-hewn man, with little learning or sophistication, but he has a courtliness about him that we have always found becoming."

"We Americans and you French are quite different people."

"So you always said," Dumond replied. "But we are becoming more like you every day, and you, in turn, are becoming more like each other. Aside from your curious ambivalence about slavery, I see little difference between other Americans and those who call themselves Yankee."

"Ah," Beede said. "And that is the reason I have come to see you, for I have come to purchase a Negro."

"It is my understanding that it is illegal to own slaves in New England," said Dumond. "Are you intending to return to Louisiana? I, for one, would welcome you, and here you can own as many slaves as you can afford."

"Not a slave," Beede said. "But it's true that I wish to purchase a Negro—a particular Negro, in fact. Her name is Louisa, and she is Randolph's wife."

"Is Randolph with you, then? Why is he not here? I would be happy to extend my hospitality to all the members of your household."

"Randolph is staying with friends," Beede said. "And he is no longer a member of my household. I gave him his freedom three years ago, and he now owns the farm adjacent to mine."

Dumond smiled. "I can imagine Randolph as a free

man," he said. "It is rather more difficult to imagine him as a farmer. He was always a house servant when he was with me."

"He is doing well," Beede said. "In fact, we help each other, and I'm indebted to him for his assistance. He came through the first growing season very successfully, and has acquired some cash money. While we lived in Washington City he married a young slave woman, and he has been saving the funds to purchase her from her owner. But when we returned to make the purchase, we found that she had already been sold. It's our belief that she was sent to one of the slave markets here in New Orleans."

"How long ago would this have been?"

"It's difficult to say," Beede replied. "We began our search in November, after our crops were in. We have the impression that she had been sold only a few months earlier. She was a house servant in Alexandria, the city across the river from Washington, and is a skilled cook and seamstress."

"So she was probably not sold as a field hand," Dumond said. "Nevertheless, that possibility cannot be ruled out entirely. Regardless of her previous servitude, her new owner may make use of her in any fashion he desires, and the need for field hands on the cotton and sugar plantations is great."

"That is our fear."

"But not your greatest fear, I expect. Not Randolph's greatest fear, at any event. Slaves cannot marry legally, of course, but that wouldn't matter a great deal to a slaveholder who considered her attractive."

"And I suppose it might not matter that she considers herself married."

"Not in the least," Dumond said. "Some owners

might even consider it their duty to have her for themselves, in the hope of breaking whatever emotional ties might linger. Or they might give her to another slave in the hope of producing new slaves."

"I admit that I don't understand the ins and outs of slavery," Beede said. "I realized when we planned our journey that I had not even visited a slave market during my years in the South."

"So you will require my assistance in some form," Dumond said. "I can see that. What would you have me do?"

"We need someone who knows the market—and *is known* in the market—to guide us in our search."

"I have not purchased a Negro for many years," Dumond said. "I daresay, however, that I can be useful to you, nevertheless. Very well. We shall begin in the morning."

Chapter 3

Something was wrong. She knew it. The land she saw around her did not resemble anything she had seen before, in Virginia or in any of the territories she had passed through on her way to this place. If she were going north, as she intended, shouldn't her surroundings begin to resemble those with which she was familiar? Surely the world at large must look much like Virginia.

There were swamps in Virginia, of course, but these were unlike any others in her experience. The trees were gnarled and twisted in grotesque shapes and draped with some sort of gray grasslike vegetation that hung from tree limbs like ghosts and swayed in the breeze, making ghostly, rustling sounds in the night. And there were other noises emanating from the darkness that sent shivers down her back—roaring and croaking as she had never heard before.

She had stuck to her original plan, sleeping in the daytime and traveling by road at night, taking to the woods at the first sound of riders approaching. Her journey, so far, had been uneventful, although it required her utmost vigilance not to be caught out when the slave catchers passed through.

But it had now been three days, her food was almost gone, and she had no idea what she would do when it finally ran out. She had heard of runaways who had survived by living off the land for months, but she had no idea how to do it for herself. Which plants in this wet, teeming jungle by the roadside were edible? She could prepare meat for cooking, if she had meat, but she had none and no idea how to find it. Nor would she know how to prepare a fire without yesterday's embers on the hearth to blow back to life.

As she thought about them, she realized that the stories of survival she had heard in the quarters had all come from slaves. That was a sobering realization; all those from whom she had heard those tales had once, briefly, been free but were free no longer. Either they had been recaptured and severely beaten for their troubles, or they had returned of their own accord, usually much thinner and hungrier than they had left and much the worse for wear.

And what about the others, who had run away but had not returned? Had they succeeded? Were they now living in freedom in the northern states, where it was rumored that slavery did not—could not—exist? Had they made their way to New Orleans, or Richmond, or some other big city, and melted into the crowds in the congested streets and alleyways, where no one who looked for them would ever find them again? Or had they, as seemed more likely at this moment, been run to ground, or starved, or killed by the bite of a cotton-mouth or rattlesnake? She had not seen one, but she had heard stories of "gators" since arriving in Louisiana. These were long lizards, the old men said, that slithered through the tall grass near the bayous and lay in wait for fugitives, preferably slaves.

It had been easy, in the fear of the moment, to take to the road, to convince herself that any change would be for the better. Now, when it was too late, when her irrevocable decision had been made, the old doubts were returning.

Dusk was falling. It was time to begin moving again. She took up her now-depleted store of food and set out once more on the road.

"There isn't much I can do here," the doctor said.

"You can tell me if it was a pistol ball that killed her," the sheriff said.

"You didn't need me to tell you that. You can see the hole in her chest, plain as I can. She surely wasn't stabbed to death, and she didn't fall and break her neck."

"I meant," the sheriff said with as much patience as he could muster, "that it wasn't a rifle or a musket, was it?"

"Oh, well, no. I don't think so. Looks like a shooting at very close range. Lots of scorching and burned powder around that hole. You must have seen that yourself.

People are always shooting each other around here, most often from real close, like this."

"Thank you, Doc. Now tell me, could she have done this to herself?"

"You mean suicide?"

"Well, yes. Or an accident."

"Where'd she dispose of the gun, then?"

"I don't know. It ain't here, but I'm guessing that's its twin over there in that case. It's a dueling pistol."

"Why'd you ask me what kind of gun it was? You knew all along."

"I thought I knew, but I like to hear it from somebody else before I go asking questions, shaking things up," the sheriff said. "If I assume this is the right gun, and it turns out later it was a rifle or musket that killed her, I can waste a lot of time looking in the wrong place and asking the wrong questions."

The doctor nodded. "I guess the dueling pistol is a little misleading. This sure weren't a duel."

"I wish it was," Schneider said. "Duels are easy enough to figure out—you got witnesses around, usually—but murders are messier things. Especially murders of old ladies who ain't hurt anybody that I'm aware of. I was just hoping I'd overlooked something."

The doctor closed his bag with a snap and stood up wearily.

"Well, this one's a murder, Conrad. You can take it from me. If she'd shot herself the gun would be by her side—maybe even in her hand. You don't need me to tell you that."

"Yeah, I know. It don't make sense, though. Nobody hated her, far as I can tell. She don't have family, to speak of. If she had a husband, that'd be one thing, but she didn't."

"No husband," the doctor said in confirmation. "There's an overseer, but I don't think he sees her very much. She let him do his job and didn't interfere much."

"That's my point," Schneider said. "Who's left to care if she lives or dies? And what're they going to care about? All she's got is this land, which is a piss-poor piece of property if ever I saw one. I don't expect she left a will. I hear there's no one left to leave things to. I can't see the motive."

"People kill people all the time around here," the doctor said. "I suppose they think they have reasons, but most of them don't make sense to anyone but themselves."

"True enough. But they're usually angry about something. That kind of killing's usually not as neat as this one. One bullet—bang—at close range, and then they leave the other gun behind, walk out the door, and go away?"

"What about her slaves? They all accounted for?"

"I got Howie out in the fields, asking around, but I don't think we'll find anybody missing. There weren't all that many left; she sold most of them a while back."

"Well, Howie told me she bought one not long ago, too. Not a field hand. Sort of a cook and housemaid. I think she sleeps down at the kitchen. She around?"

"I don't know," Schneider said. "I didn't think about a woman maybe doing this. I'd better ask Howie about her."

"Don't take a lot of strength to pull a trigger," the

doctor said. "Especially if the gun's already loaded and primed."

"You're right," Schneider said, rising from the floor. "She sleeps down at the kitchen, you think? What's her name?"

"Eloise, Louise, something like that maybe. You ready for me to take the body away?"

"Go ahead," Schneider said. "I'm tired of looking at her. Let me know if you learn anything else I can use."

"Con?"

"Yeah?"

"I just remembered. Louisa. The new cook's name is Louisa."

"Then I hope she's guilty," Schneider said. "Louisa was my wife's name."

Chapter 4

It wasn't a long walk from Pierre Dumond's house on Rue Royale to the slave market. Randolph joined them that next morning, and Dumond led them at a brisk pace down the street to a high-walled brick building near the river, almost in the shadow of the cathedral. It had rained during the night, and the street had become a muddy bisque that spotted their trouser legs and congealed on their boots. Dumond halted the little party—Beede and Randolph—just at the entrance to the first market building.

"If you would permit me, I shall serve as your voice in your transaction," Dumond said. "Since I do not know the woman you are seeking, however, I must rely on your eyes to find her. For safety's sake, Randolph should pose as a slave."

"That is satisfactory," Beede said.

They entered a large room swarming with white men in high hats and black frock coats. Beede, who had diligently avoided the place during his years in New Orleans, was astonished at the activity. It reminded him of the riverbank of the previous morning. The city was known as an important port for cotton, sugar, grains, and a variety of manufactured and agricultural products, but clearly the human chattel trade also was important to the New Orleans economy.

He counted more than a hundred men, women, and children awaiting buyers, cheek by jowl around the perimeter of the room, men at one side, women and children at the other. As they strolled past the huddle of women, Dumond would glance at Beede as if to ascertain whether the woman they sought was present. Beede, who had seen Louisa only a few times, several years earlier, would glance, in turn, toward Randolph, who would solemnly shake his head.

"No luck?" Dumond said when they had completed their circuit. "Well, on to the next, then."

Systematically, they approached the establishment of each trading firm and carefully inspected each woman in the showroom, but without success. There was no shortage of women—or men—to scrutinize, nor was there a shortage of potential buyers. At each stop, the likeliest candidates were inspected eagerly by an enthusiastic coterie of men, who poked and prodded, thrust hands into mouths, pinched breasts, and ran fingers over and into places that Beede had always thought to be private.

The women tolerated this handling without protest, for the most part, although an occasional grimace could be seen when the inspection became overzealous. They bore the familiarity in grim silence, however, knowing full well the consequences of complaining. Beede was sickened and said as much to Randolph.

"This is the usual practice in the market," Randolph said in a low voice, so Dumond could not hear him. "I was here only once before, when I was sold as a young boy with my mother. The white men did much the same thing to her. Fortunately, I was purchased soon afterward. M'sieur Dumond was not a bad master, as such men go, and my life was not as onerous as it might have been otherwise."

"And your mother?"

Randolph shook his head. "I never saw her again. She was purchased before me, and I fear the worst. The white man who bought her had, I am sure, lascivious plans for her. That was twenty years ago, or perhaps more. She's dead now, I suspect."

"This was a fruitless exercise," Dumond said that evening after they had retreated to the house on Rue Royale. "I suspected that would be the case, however, and in any event this does not exhaust our alternatives."

"I can see why you have not bought additional slaves in many years," Beede said. "Does it not render you heartsick to see such an example of greed in action? I could not bring myself to engage in a business of such a foul nature as this, even once."

"I have no need of additional servants," Dumond said. "My household is quite large enough for my needs. Otherwise, I might well be in the market with an eye toward purchase. There are certain hard attributes to the business, as there are in any business, but it's nothing from which a man should recoil. We are all required to perform distasteful acts on occasion."

"The buying and selling of human flesh seems not so much distasteful as immoral," Beede said.

"Quite the contrary. Think about what you have seen today," Dumond said.

"I have been doing so."

"Did you see unhappiness? Did you see frowns? Weeping? Did you not see slaves dancing, and playing fiddles so that other slaves might dance? On the contrary, the atmosphere was festive, joyful."

"An act," Beede said. "A masquerade directed by the traders."

"Undoubtedly," Dumond said. "But why? Why do they put on such airs if they are truly miserable, as you seem to believe?"

"Fear," said Beede. "Fear of beatings, or torture. Perhaps worse."

"Fear in some cases," Dumond agreed. "But surely not in every instance. No, it is in their own best interest to create a good impression with a buyer. If their owners are favorably disposed, the slaves will receive better treatment at their hands. It is to their mutual benefit."

"I'm sorry, Pierre. I can't believe that slaves enjoy slavery."

"Of course they do not. Who among us enjoys every aspect of our lives, *mon ami?* I say only that they *do* enjoy some parts of their lives. They must work hard, of course. There is no escaping that. But on the other hand, they are spared the responsibility of ensuring their own survival. It is a hard life, but we all—all of us—have hard lives."

Chapter 5

Saturday, December 23, 1837
Tomkins Farm
Warrensboro, New Hampshire

Dear Mr. Beede,

*It has now been more than a month since we parted
company, and I find myself wondering how your
search is faring. I hope that your efforts are meeting
with success and that you have met already with
dear Mr. Randolph's wife. Perhaps you are, even
now, on your way back to your friends and to your
farm. If so, this letter may not reach you until after
you return, in which event I will be able to deliver
my communication to you in person.*

I apologize for not writing sooner, for it had been my intention to do so long before now. I find it difficult to express on paper what is in my heart, a circumstance I had never considered until now. With the friends of my childhood I seem to have no difficulty conveying my thoughts, whether in person or in writing, but I come up against an impediment when writing to those with whom I have not long been acquainted. So it seems to be when writing to you.

And yet, we are hardly strangers! Although our acquaintance has been short, we have experienced many things together, and I feel that I know you better than I know many friends of longer duration. And if this is true, why should I be shy or reticent in my correspondence with you? I confess that I do not understand my own feelings in this regard.

You shall be pleased to hear that all is well at your farm. Father and I rode out that way late last week and found everything to be in order. Mr. Randolph's property was in rather less order, but he of course has had rather less time than you in which to put things aright.

Do you anticipate returning in time for planting in the spring? Father says it might be possible to place one or two of our hired hands on your property—yours and Mr. Randolph's—if needed, in order to obtain an early start in the coming season. You may wish to discuss this matter with Mr. Randolph and let me know at your earliest opportunity.

Hoping to hear from you soon, I remain

Your friend,
Deborah Tomkins

"Good news?" asked Pierre Dumond.

Beede refolded the letter and placed it in his breast pocket. "Merely a communication from a neighbor in New Hampshire. She and her father are looking after our farms—Randolph's and mine—during our absence. Not that there's much to go wrong at this time of year. It's typically a matter of feeding the livestock and milking the cows—and neither of us has many animals."

Dumond, however, caught the reference Beede had attempted to hide.

"She?" he said. "Do I understand that you are seeing a young lady? It isn't customary for someone to volunteer to look after another person's farm unless a close relationship already exists."

"In New England, matters are handled differently," Beede said. "Our farms are small, and our villages are close together. None of us can be self-sufficient on our own, the way your southern planters can. We have neither the arable land nor the men."

"Meaning," Dumond said, "that you have no slaves to assist you and likely could not support them if you had. I take your point; nevertheless, I am intrigued by the possibility you are so carefully avoiding: Is there a new young lady in my friend Josiah's life?"

"I—"

"Please do not misunderstand me," Dumond added hastily. "I am happy for you, if that is the case. I loved Adrienne as a daughter as much as you loved her as a wife, but life must go on. She has been gone for many years, and you are still a young and vigorous man. It is not right that you should be alone."

"And what about Pierre Dumond?"

"Ah, well," Dumond said. "Perhaps I, too, will wed

again, if the opportunity arises. I was married far longer than you, however, and I am also much older. Margarethe and I had three children, of whom only Adrienne lived past the age of three. As one grows older it becomes more difficult to come to terms with disappointment."

"I understand that," Beede said. "Sometimes I feel much older than I know myself to be. The brevity of our time together—Adrienne and I—is difficult for me to come to terms with."

"Perhaps," Dumond said, stirring the fireplace embers. "But you must try to do so. Is this young lady someone whom you might consider as a wife?"

"I don't know," Beede said, more truthfully than he had intended.

They were in the sitting room of Dumond's house. Breakfast had been consumed, and the young serving girl had cleared away the dishes. They sipped café au lait and awaited the arrival of Dumond's first custom of the day. Beede and Randolph had made plans to meet later in the morning, but for the moment Beede had no pressing business. It was pleasant to sit with an old friend and sip coffee in the frosty morning, to gaze outside at the haze and drizzle and give thanks that one had no need to go out into it just yet. Northerners tended to believe that the southern states—and New Orleans, in particular—were oppressive, sweltering hotboxes in which human beings were fortunate to survive at all. They should come at Carnival or at Christmas, he thought, and experience for themselves just how cold the South could be in winter.

"So this is a matter to which you have given some thought," Dumond said.

The coffee was as good as he remembered. He sipped it slowly, as much to buy a moment before responding as to savor the brew.

"Yes," he said, finally. "Yes, I have."

He had, in fact, given the matter considerable thought. On their last evening in Warrensboro, he had gone to say his farewells to Deborah and her family, who had graciously volunteered their services to look after their farms—his and Randolph's—during their absence. He had planned only a brief visit before parting, but it had lasted well into the night.

He had been received warmly, and the talk was pleasant. The entire family had participated, and the house had resounded with laughter. As he took his leave, Deborah had accompanied him to—and through—the doorway, although the night was cold, as it always was in November.

They had stood facing each other and talked for some time longer. He had been astonished at how much they had found to discuss, there in the chill. None of it was crucial, and yet everything was crucial. He shivered, but he would not let her see it for fear that she would take that as an excuse to break off their conversation and return indoors. Surprisingly, she seemed as reluctant as he to end their tête-à-tête.

"I hope your journey will be successful," she said finally.

"As do I," he said. "Randolph deserves some happiness in his life. He has dreamed of a reunion with his wife for many years.

"I pray that you will return to us," she said. "And that you will not be seduced once more by the pleasures of New Orleans, about which I have heard many stories."

"There is little danger of that," he said, smiling. "New Orleans is certainly a seductive city, but I have a responsibility to Randolph. Randolph could not live again in New Orleans, where he would constantly be in danger of being kidnapped and sold back into slavery. I must see to it that he returns safely."

"As well as yourself," she said.

"I'm in no danger," he said.

"I pray that it will always be true," she said. And she raised herself on her toes and kissed him.

It was a brief kiss, and chaste, but it was a kiss on the lips. His arms encircled her, quite without thinking, and he held her close for a moment, savoring the closeness and the warmth of her young body.

He knew she had thought of him as a prospective suitor—indeed, she had told him so—but he had been certain that her inclination would change as she grew older. He knew he was not a prize. Eligible, certainly, but at age thirty-eight too old and too phlegmatic for a young woman in her early twenties. His only qualification was that he could provide a comfortable home for her. This was not an inconsequential consideration, of course, but he was certain that other men could do as well, or better, and be possessed, moreover, with the passion of youth. He feared that his passion—of which there had been little enough—had long been spent.

But the kiss was spontaneous and unexpected and remained with him long after they had parted and he had begun the walk back to his farm.

It had not always been thus. When he had met Adrienne, in the heady days that followed the magnificent, unexpected victory at the Battle of New Orleans, he had truly been young and vigorous. He had a reputation for heroism, misplaced though it was, and young women flocked to him—none more so than the beautiful young daughter of Pierre Dumond.

He had met Adrienne when he was a mere fifteen, and they had married when he was barely twenty-five. The marriage had lasted five years until Adrienne had died from childbed fever, but by then they had lost the ardor and intimacy with which they had begun their lives together. Beede blamed himself for that; Adrienne had been young and impressionable and had thought she was marrying a hero, when in fact he was nothing of the sort. She had learned the truth to her disappointment, and the truth had been very hard to bear.

Was he now setting Deborah up for disappointment as well? He had never been able to disabuse others of his reputation for heroism, which often led to disenchantment when the painful truth eventually became apparent. A reputation for valor was difficult to maintain and equally difficult to shed, and it led almost inevitably to disillusionment.

All told, he thought as he arrived at his house, public acclaim had proven itself more a burden than a benefit.

Chapter 6

It was growing more difficult to make progress in the swamp. The ground was becoming softer, and her footsteps created a suction that made it harder to lift her feet with every step. At times she wished she had been taught to swim; but then she would think of the creatures that lived in that tea-brown water and thank her stars that she could not. An inability to swim, however, would leave her vulnerable to the dogs, if they were to pick up her scent.

How far was she from the plantation house? Three days' walk—three good days' walk. It might be far enough that the patrols would give up the search for her. Or it might be that she had not yet left the widow's property. Farms here seemed to go on forever.

And when she thought more about it, she realized they would continue to search for her. She was not merely a fugitive; she also was property. Widow Hawkins would send a search party to recover her investment, and she would not give up. She *could* not give up.

A whiff of wood smoke caught her nostrils, reminding her that the sky had been growing lighter for some time. The plantations were awakening, and the fields would soon be busy. It was time for her to take to the woods, to go to ground.

But mixed with the smell of wood smoke was the smell of bacon.

She hadn't realized how hungry she was. Heedless of the danger, she followed her nose until she came upon a clearing where an old woman was tending a laundry kettle in front of a small kitchen house. The woman had her back turned, facing the big house perhaps fifty yards away. The bacon aroma came from the cookhouse.

She knew the bacon would be meant for the big house. This old woman, who probably was the cook, would receive none. Bacon was for white folks; corn mush was for slaves.

But the aroma was almost more than Louisa could bear. She stifled a heartfelt groan, closed her eyes, and attempted to block out the dull ache that was spreading across her forehead. Her eyes opened again when she heard a woman's voice close at hand.

"Yes'm. I hears you. I'll just be pourin' out this wash water!"

Terrified, Louisa stared out through the underbrush as the old woman came nearer, fairly wrestling the fire-blackened pot toward the very place where she lay hidden. Louisa dared not move, for any movement would draw attention to her hiding place. Instead she willed herself to disappear and prayed that she would not be discovered.

The old woman was on top of her, now half-carrying, half-dragging the washtub the last few feet toward the edge of the clearing. When it seemed to Louisa that she was about to be found, the woman straightened and tipped the tub on its side. The water spattered into the brush and spilled over Louisa's feet and legs before running into the swamp behind her. It was, as she feared, scalding hot, and she bit her lip to keep from screaming.

"Tansy! You get in here!"

"Yes'm!" the woman shouted. She stood up to go, and Louisa almost sighed in relief.

Perhaps she actually did. In any event, the old woman leaned over the bush she hid behind and said, softly but distinctly: "Stay put! I'll be back shortly so you stay right where you are!"

"We've searched all over, Con. She ain't here," Howie said.

"If I was her, I wouldn't of stuck around, neither," Schneider said.

They were standing on the veranda of the big house watching the doctor supervise the removal of the body of the widow Hawkins. Two slaves, borrowed from the field, carried the woman's corpse and laid her gently in the bed of a buckboard wagon. Her face was covered by a sheet, of course; nevertheless, the field hands studiously averted their gaze from the woman as they stretched her out on a bed of straw.

"So I guess she must of done it, huh?" Howie said.

"I guess," Schneider said. He strolled over to the wagon and watched the loading.

"Rigor's passing," the doctor said. "I guess that'd make it, oh, about twenty-four hours since she died. If she was a late sleeper, she might have never woke up. Before she was killed, I mean."

"Makes sense. Ain't no sign of a struggle. Just that one shot, in just the right place."

"It's funny, though," the doctor said. "Dueling pistols come in twos. Where's the other one?"

"Might be our killer's still got it," Schneider said.

Howie had remained on the veranda during this conversation. Schneider walked back to join him.

"Guess you should take your boys and scout around, see if you can find her," he said. "She's had a day or so head start on us, but she ain't from around here. She won't know the country very well, I don't suppose. And see if the overseer has some ideas where she mighta gone."

"Well, that's another thing," Howie said. "We can't find him neither. I'm wonderin' if they took off together."

"White man and a nigger woman?"

"Wouldn't be the first time," Howie said. "The servants say she was uncommon pretty, and he'd been hangin' around her a lot. They figure he'd been puttin' it to her some."

"Might be the reason she ran away," Schneider said. "Don't make sense that she'd run off with him, though."

"You ain't been here long enough," Howie said. "You think white folks and black folks don't ever get together, 'cause you ain't seen it for yourself. Down

here, it happens a lot, and with slaves it happens a
whole lot. Hell, it can mean the difference between
workin' in the fields and livin' in the big house. Lot of
them girls will fight each other for the chance."

Schneider sighed. "All right, Howie. I'll take your
word for it. Let's see what we can find. If we find 'em
together, that'll make things a lot simpler for all of us."

Howie trotted off eagerly to organize a search party,
and Schneider watched gloomily as Howie disappeared
behind the outbuildings.

Howie was right, Schneider thought. He hadn't been
long in Louisiana, and he was finding the adjustment
difficult. In Illinois, there were hardly any Negroes, and
there were no slaves. White folks and black folks
mostly stuck to their own. Down here, they mixed together in a hundred different ways, and everything got
jumbled up together. You had black slaves and freeborn
blacks, and free blacks who had been manumitted by
their owners or who had worked their way out of slavery, often by hiring themselves out to others with their
owners' permission. You had runaways who had managed to make it to a city and lose themselves in the
crowd until they could obtain forged papers. Then you
had your mulattoes, and your quadroons and your oc-
toroons—determined by how much white blood they
supposedly had in their veins—and some of them were
free and some were slaves. On top of that, there were
even a few white indentured servants, immigrants and
native-born alike, who were practically slaves themselves for a specified period of time.

And up in New Orleans, he had been told, Creole
gentlemen often took colored mistresses—young free
colored women—and set them up in their own houses,

paying them a stipend, often educating their children, sometimes even abandoning their wives and families to take up housekeeping with their concubines. Often these women were remembered in their protectors' wills, despite the outraged objections of the presumed heirs.

Schneider had no strong opinions about slavery one way or the other. Moving to the South had been, for him, strictly a matter of economics; he was a peace officer and went where he was needed. But he wondered often how a system such as this could survive much longer. Indeed, he wondered how it had survived as long as it had.

But there were no signs—that he could detect—that the system was dying. In fact, it was growing stronger. The legislature was always tightening the screws on slaves, making it more difficult for owners to free their servants, requiring that freed slaves leave the state (and their families), and further restricting the ability of slaves to throw off their shackles.

Well, he thought, it wasn't his concern. He had no slaves, personally, and no desire to acquire them. In truth, he couldn't afford slaves and doubted that he ever would.

He stepped back in the house and looked once again into the room where Esther Hawkins had lain. Although her body had been removed, the faint smell of death lingered in the air. He could still see the indentation of her body on the bedclothes.

Chapter 7

Beede, Dumond, and Randolph returned to the markets the following day. Having established to their satisfaction that the woman they were seeking was not present, they now set out to determine whether she had passed through the markets earlier and, if so, where she might have been sent.

It was a frustrating and time-consuming process. Slave dealers had little incentive to help a noncustomer locate a slave in whom they no longer had a financial interest. Beede solved the dilemma through the simple expedient of bribery.

Even so, it was a tedious exercise. It was not until nearly a week had passed that a dealer came upon an entry in his ledger.

"Louisa, I believe you said?" the dealer said, looking

up from his books. "This is, perhaps, the entry you seek."

He pointed out the notations as they gathered around him. "She was acquired from a broker who passed through here in September with a coffle that he had assembled back east: Virginia, the Carolinas, and one or two from northern Georgia."

"That would fit with what we know," Beede said. "What do you remember about the girl?"

"Many slaves are traded here," he said. "It's difficult to remember all of them." He peered carefully at the notation. "This one I believe I remember, however. She was light-skinned, rather like a quadroon, as I recall. Quite young and pretty, more like a fancy than a domestic servant, if you know what I mean."

"Where is she now?" Randolph said.

The dealer glared at him for a moment, clearly offended by this Negro's effrontery, but he answered quickly enough. "She was sold, of course. Girls like that don't stay on the market long, and she was no exception. Let's see who bought her."

He bent over the ledger and peered closely at the page.

"I'm sorry about this," he said. "This isn't my hand. Looks like Felix's, my assistant. I can't make it out. Felix!"

The young man who appeared at the door was about seventeen, Beede guessed, with thinning blond hair that emphasized his sloping forehead.

"I can't read your writing," the dealer said to him. "You'll have to read this entry for me."

The young man leaned over his employer's shoulder.

"Why, that's M'sieur Balfour, sir. He bought that high-yellow girl, Louisa."

"Are you certain of this?" Beede asked.

"Oh, yes, sir," Felix replied. "Not easy to forget that transaction. He paid in specie 'stead of scrip. Very unusual these days. Wish *all* our customers paid in coin."

"That *is* uncommon," Pierre Dumond said. "Since President Jackson ordered that federal land sales must be paid for in specie, there has been a terrible shortage of gold and silver coin. The banks can't keep enough in their vaults to meet the need."

"Of course, M'sieur Balfour is employed at the mint," the trader said. "If anyone should have specie to spare, it should be he."

"But he's merely an employee," Felix pointed out. "And he's not a wealthy man, by any means. Look at the way he dresses, that hat that sags like a willow branch."

"Nevertheless, who should have greater access to coin than an employee of the mint," the trader said. "And I must remind you that it is not appropriate to disparage a customer's manner of dress. Times have been hard for many since the banks began to fail."

"Yes, sir," Felix said. "Will there be anything else? I should be getting back to the trading floor."

"No, go ahead," the trader said. He turned to Beede. "M'sieur Balfour, as Felix has said, works at the new United States Mint on Esplanade. I was unaware that they were actually minting coinage there, although I know they were supposed to begin sometime this year. In any event, you should be able to find him there. He's in charge of supervising the coinage, I believe."

"How will we know him?" Beede asked.

"Why, you should *ask* for him," the trader said. "He won't be difficult to identify, in any event. Felix was right about his bedraggled top hat, and he also goes everywhere with a gold-handled cane, which he often uses to clear his way on the street. You'll know him, sir. Believe me, you'll know him."

Chapter 8

Louisa waited.

She dared not move, although her crouching position grew almost unbearably painful. She alleviated the agony from time to time by slowly stretching one leg in front of her and then the other, not having the courage to stand and not being entirely certain that she would be able to do so if she tried.

As she waited, she wondered—in silence—if she were making the correct choice. The old woman who had spoken so furtively had seemed confident and firm—so much so that Louisa had obeyed without a second thought, although every instinct cried out for flight. And not merely flight, but desperate, headlong flight.

But she had been waiting now for—how long? Time had very little meaning to her under the best of circumstances. Her life had always been ruled by her work-load, and not by the hours of the day: wake in the morning and work until dark, then work some more, then sleep, then rise and work again. She could tell the time of day—roughly—by the sun, but clocks had no meaning to her, and no utility. Others—her various mistresses—might look at a clock and announce that it was now noon, or three o'clock in the afternoon. To Louisa, there were only two times of day—work time and sleep time—and one was infinitely longer than the other.

But she could see through the treetops that the sun was quite high in the sky, which meant that she had been hiding here for most of the day. She began gathering her strength and courage for her inevitable flight when she heard the old woman's voice once more.

"It's safe now. You can come out. My mistress just gone to town and won't be back for a while. Can you stand?"

She couldn't. She rose almost to an upright position when her knees buckled and she went sprawling on the ground. The old woman chuckled and extended her hand.

"Figgered you might have some trouble, long as you been scrunched up. Let me help you."

"Thank you."

With the old woman's arm around her waist, Louisa tottered toward the house. Her legs gradually regained their effectiveness, but she was almost to the house before she felt strong enough to walk on her own.

"Figgered you was hungry, too, considerin' how long you been on the road, so I fixed up a little somethin' for you. It ain't much, but I reckon it's more than you had for a spell."

The old woman helped her to a chair in the kitchen house. Louisa sank gratefully into it as she thought about the lies she would have to tell to explain her presence here.

"Thank you again," she began. "I 'spect you're wondering who I am and what I'm doing here."

The old woman cackled. "Honey, I *knows* who you is, and I knows where you come from. Ain't a slave for miles around don't know who you is and why you runnin'. You famous, chile. You that Louisa, killed ol' lady Hawkins and her overseer, that Travis, over to Twin Oaks."

Louisa put down the wooden bowl of cornmeal mush from which she had been eating.

"Killed?"

"That's what usual happens when you shoot a body with a pistol. Of course, they don't know for certain about that Travis 'cause they cain't find him yet. He plumb disappeared." The old woman cackled again.

"I never killed her," Louisa said. Her heart was pounding now so loud she thought the woman could hear it. "Not her, not nobody. You gots to believe me."

"Don't *matter* whether I believe you. Ain't nobody goin' to wonder whether an ol' nigger like me thinks you done it or not. It's that white sheriff you goin' to have to convince, if he ever finds you. And he's lookin'. He surely is."

The hunger was replaced by knot in the pit of her stomach. "How *can* I convince him?" she said. "I didn't even know she was dead. I can't let him find me."

She struggled to rise from her chair, but the old woman put a hand on her shoulder and gently pressed her down again.

"Don't you worry none," she said. "He ain't goin' to find you, leastwise not here. We gonna get you some help, a place to hide out for a spell. You just eat up your food and let ol' Tansy worry about gettin' you away from here safe."

"The way I see it," Howie said, "the girl kills the old lady and then she kills the overseer—Dudley Travis, his name is, accordin' to the field hands—and then lights out for New Orleans, quick as she can."

"Maybe," Schneider said as the two men rode slowly home. "Or maybe Travis killed the old lady, and the girl runs away because she's afraid we'll blame it on her. Or maybe Travis kills the old lady and runs away with the girl. Or maybe Travis kills the old lady *and* the girl, and then *he* skedaddles. There's a million ways this could of gone, looks to me."

"If he killed the girl, what'd he do with the body? She ain't here."

"And if the girl killed Travis, what'd she do with *his* body? She was, what, a little over five feet, you said? And he was five-seven or so. She musta been a right strong little girl to haul away a body like that. You better get your boys looking for a trail, drag marks, or something."

"We looked already. Didn't find none."

"All right, then." Tired of rehashing a discussion he had been having in one form or another for three days, Schneider turned away from his deputy to stare off into the swamp.

Something was not right, he thought. Hell, a lot of things weren't right. This was no crime of passion in the usual way of things—indeed, he doubted that old Esther Hawkins had inspired passion for many years, or had desired to. From what he had heard, there hadn't been much passion even when old Elmer Hawkins had been alive, and he had been dead too many years for even a relic of those days to have continued to smolder.

Of course, there were men whose passions were so deep-seated and so twisted that they were hidden even from themselves, and who might have killed their victim while appeasing those passions. But Esther Hawkins had not been violated or molested in any way that Schneider could see. Merely murdered with one clean shot to the chest, fired from close range.

And shot, moreover, with a dueling pistol, a delicate and exceedingly unreliable weapon that often misfired and sometimes exploded in the user's face. Schneider knew of occasions when two parties departed on an affair of honor, and both parties subsequently returned alive—often wounded, missing an eye, or bereft of some other favored part of their anatomy—but unquestionably alive. He suspected that many duelists selected pistols as their weapons of choice *because* so many things could go wrong when pistols were involved. A good swordsman possessed an immeasurable advantage over an unskilled adversary; pistols largely negated the skill factor. An unskilled man might be killed in a duel involving guns, but so might his better-prepared adversary.

The discovery of the dueling pistol worried him. Such guns were smoothbore, muzzle-loading, flintlock instruments designed for only one thing: to kill another human being face to face at close range, with a single shot.

Schneider had little use for pistols. They combined the worst elements of guns and swords, requiring you to close the distance with your adversary as you would in a sword fight, but depriving you of the accuracy and reliability of a sword. In a pistol duel, that might be the point: to introduce a degree of uncertainty so that the encounter would not be quite the unrelenting slaughter it might otherwise be. Indeed, it was the element of chance—and *only* the element of chance, he thought—that continued to make dueling a viable alternative for the settlement of disputes. If one desired to murder another, a blunt, heavy object might do as well.

Perhaps the dueling pistol was chosen merely because it was at hand. But that made no sense, either. Women did not fight duels and so would have no need of such a pistol, and probably would not know how to load it, prime it, or aim it. It might have belonged to her husband, of course, but he had died more than a decade ago. The gun could not have remained loaded and ready for firing for so long a time in this steamy downriver jungle.

Clearly, there was still too much he did not know, and he promised himself that he would learn more.

Chapter 9

Balfour's office was on the third floor of the mint. Beede and Dumond followed a wobbly old slave down an echoing corridor to a room hardly larger than the cabin of the little merchant ship Beede had arrived aboard. The man they sought was seated with his back to the door, poring carefully over a stack of gold coins. He turned, startled, when his visitors entered.

"It is customary to knock before entering a room," he said. He peered closely at Beede. "I know you, I believe."

He did, Beede realized, as a wave of distaste swept through him. The man before them—who now had clearly placed them as well—was none other than the man with whom he had had an altercation on the river levee.

"If there was any man I had hoped that I would never

meet again, it was you," Balfour said. "Have you come to lord it over me with your Yankee airs, sir? Am I never to be free of you?"

"It is a shock equally unpleasant to me, sir," Beede said. "I had not realized that I would come into your presence again."

"Well, what is it that you want? I am a busy man. I have no time to waste in idle chitchat—even pleasant chitchat, which I am certain this would not be."

"Nor for me, m'sieur. It is necessity that brings me here, not preference."

"Then come in and sit down. Let us make our encounter no more unpleasant than is required." He motioned them to chairs and swung to face them.

"I am Josiah Beede," Beede began. "And this is my friend and father-in-law, Pierre Dumond. We have come to see you because we believe you may be able to assist us in finding a young colored woman."

"Where is your nigger?" Balfour said. "Wouldn't it have been sensible to send him on this errand?"

"Randolph had other responsibilities this morning," Beede said carefully. "He could not join us." In fact, Randolph was spending the morning inquiring among the household staffs in the Creole houses of the city, something neither Beede nor Dumond could effectively do.

"And why do you believe that I could help you find this woman, even if I chose to do so? For the sake of friendship? I would be reluctant to presume upon our relationship, such as it is, if I were in your shoes."

It was Dumond who chose to break the impasse. "The girl we seek is a slave named Louisa. We were told that you had purchased her a few months ago, and we hope to purchase her from you."

Balfour laughed. "And do you think that I would sell her to you? Even if I owned her, which I do not? I would as soon sell her to an Irishman."

Dumond shook his head sadly. "I do not know the nature of your disagreement with Mr. Beede," he said. "But I wonder that you are prepared to sacrifice a commercial advantage over what can only have been a momentary altercation. Mr. Beede has been in the city only a few days, hardly long enough to have provoked such enmity."

Balfour considered this.

"I suppose you are correct," he said at last. "There would be little if any advantage to me, in any event. I have no interest in the girl; I acted merely as an agent in the transaction."

"On whose behalf?"

"I acted for a neighbor, who required a servant who would be at home in the kitchen. I found the girl at one of the local markets, and she seemed ideal for that purpose. She assured me that she could cook and had had many years of experience."

"Why did your neighbor not act for himself?" Beede asked.

"Because *she* could not," Balfour said. "A slave market is no place for a woman. She is a widow, whose husband has been deceased for many years. She has no living kin, I believe. I felt that it was incumbent upon me to act in her stead rather than to oblige her to seek the assistance of a stranger, who might take advantage of her vulnerability."

"Very noble," Beede said.

The sarcasm was lost on Balfour, who nodded his head enthusiastically. "I felt better for assisting her," he said. "One should always help those who are weak and powerless when it is within one's capacity to do so. I have always believed this."

Beede refrained from mentioning that Louisa, as a slave, was weaker and far less powerful than her new mistress, feeling it to be a distinction that Balfour would not understand.

"Where might we find this widow?" Dumond asked. "We should like to speak to her."

"Her name is Esther Hawkins, and she lives only thirty miles or so downstream from the city. I will write out directions for you."

Beede, Randolph, and Dumond talked well into the night, discussing these new developments and what they might mean. Randolph had returned at sunset, clearly frustrated and tired but with no news to report that would compensate for his efforts. They agreed in the end that Beede and Randolph would follow Balfour's directions and seek Louisa at the plantation Balfour had described. Beede had hoped that Dumond would accompany them, but he declined.

"I have neglected my business too long," he said. "In any event, you will not need my assistance. You know the girl, and I do not."

By this time it was dark, and Randolph agreed (with great reluctance) to remain at Dumond's house for the night so that they could leave at first light and catch an early boat. The two men shared a bed in what they both

recognized had been Adrienne's room. For Beede, it
was a restless night.

Early the next morning they boarded a sternwheeler
bound downstream. The air was chilly, and Beede
would have been happy to take seats inside, but Randolph would not be welcomed there. So they stood at
the deck rail clad in the heavy winter coats they had
been wearing on their departure from New Hampshire
nearly two months earlier, and were none too warm despite them.

Here in this region a special emphasis was placed on
access to the river, which meant that every plantation
was laid out in a way that provided river frontage—
enough riverbank to allow each farm a landing and a
mail drop. Because of the river's wayward, meandering
course, each section of waterfront was narrow indeed;
the land then fanned out from the landing, with the big
house some yards inland, often barely visible from the
water. The slave quarters, often as not, would be situ-
ated even farther out of sight from the river, in part because they were the least attractive and impressive
features of every plantation compound, in part because
a slave who had to pass the big house to escape via the
river would likely think twice before making the attempt, and because it was felt that slaves didn't need a
beautiful view the way their masters did.

Somewhere back away from the river, he knew,
would be a road of some sort. They would need to find
it before they left this place; if they were unable to purchase Louisa, their chances of escaping by boat—a
strong young Negro man and a beautiful young Negro
woman assisted by a single white man—would not be
good.

Curious that he had not thought of this earlier, when some sort of precautions—what sort, he could not imagine—might still have been taken.

Randolph turned to him with an eager smile. "I've tried not to raise my hopes about this trip," he said. "But I confess that my excitement is building. We have traveled nearly ten miles, by my calculations, and in another twenty or so we should be approaching the place we seek. Soon I shall see Louisa again."

"If our information is correct," Beede said, "and if this is, indeed, where she has been sent. This is something more than we know at present."

"It's the right place," Randolph said. "I'm certain of it. I can feel it. I fancy that I can even feel her presence close at hand. This will be a joyous day for me! I know it!"

Beede tried to join in his friend's happiness, but he could not. He hoped that Randolph's instincts were right. His own instincts were telling him something quite different.

"It's a beautiful day!" Randolph shouted, and several white passengers turned, startled, and smiled.

Beede could almost hear their thoughts: Slavery cannot be wrong if a carefree young Negro man can express such joy in the presence of his master. Could a northern Negro, ostensibly free, be as happy as this young darkie who stands at the rail with his marse, exulting in the excitement of traveling on a steamboat down the Mississippi?

Beede knew their thoughts and wished that he could disabuse them of their mistaken notions. "It's not like that!" he wanted to say. "This man is free, and he is happy because he's on his way to free the woman he loves, so she also may experience a happy life—a far happier life—in the North. You don't know! You just don't know!"

But he said nothing, unwilling to open an issue that could not be resolved in the time they had available.

He glanced instead at his friend's jubilant face. Then he leaned on the deck railing once more and watched the endless riverbank as it crept past in the morning light.

The sternwheeler churned onward.

Chapter 10

At the first opportunity after he and Randolph had arrived in New Orleans, Beede had borrowed a carriage from his host and had ridden to Chalmette. It was the one place in New Orleans, save the Dumond home, to which he felt an attachment—the place at which his life had been changed irrevocably.

He took the river road, which was the most direct route. It took him past more of the curious pie-slice plantations that characterized the watery bayou world of southern Louisiana. Dumond, who had fought at Chalmette with a Creole militia contingent, had accompanied him.

They had arrived eventually at Rodriguez Canal, dry once again after all these years, and the remains of the mud rampart on its western side. Long before the battle, the canal had been a millrace, but by 1815 it had been overrun by silt. The defenders had spent much of the first day deepening and widening the trench to serve as an obstacle to the invading army.

"What do you remember of that day?" Dumond asked as they stood looking out over the plantation fields.

"Very little," Beede admitted. "I was young and frightened, and I had lost my brother in the first few minutes of the battle."

"The main part of the battle lasted, perhaps, merely half an hour," Dumond said. "I was to the left of where we stand, near the marshes, working on a gun crew. And as I watched, a curious thing happened. A battalion of Highlanders began marching diagonally across the battlefield—from the river toward our entrenchment. They had to march directly across the line of fire, and of course they were slaughtered by our guns. Hardly any remained standing by the time they reached their destination. I have often wondered who ordered such a foolhardy maneuver."

"I didn't see that," Beede said. "They must have been quite brave."

"They were Highlanders. It is not necessary to add that they were brave."

"What else do you remember?"

"I remember that I was on sentry duty the night before the battle when a commotion occurred behind the British lines. It was all conducted in whispers, so I couldn't make out what was said, but there was much running around. Later that night I heard digging. The sound was coming from the swamp, just inland from the line of battle. I was too far away to see clearly what was happening, but it went on for some time in the hours just before dawn. I thought perhaps they were digging siege works, and so we fired a round or two in that direction, as a means of discouraging them."

"Did you investigate in daylight?"

"By daylight, the British were upon us. I went back a day or so after the battle, but apparently the digging had been covered over and disguised. I've often wondered what was buried there, for I'm sure they were burying something."

They stood on the spot from which fifteen-year-old Josiah had watched in mounting panic as wave after wave of red-coated British regulars marched relentlessly toward the ragged band of Americans. The British had carried fascines—bundles of sugarcane sticks used for building fortifications—and ladders for scaling the canal and climbing the rampart. Beede remembered the fear that had grown in the pit of his stomach as he watched the battle-hardened army advancing relentlessly across the stubble of sugarcane. These were the troops who had fought the great Napoleon only months before, and they were marching toward him—him!—rank upon rigid rank.

Seth was with him then. His brother was older by two years, and Josiah had depended on his superior knowledge and experience. Then, suddenly, Seth was no longer with him, killed by a British musket ball as he pleaded with Josiah to take shelter.

He had known immediately that Seth's death was on his head. In a frenzy of rage and shame, he had seized the rifle of a nearby Kentuckian, who, being dead, had no further use of it, and fired at the oncoming horde.

Firing and reloading relentlessly, he had continued until he had exhausted his ammunition, whereupon he had found another bag of cartridges in the possession of another dead American and resumed his onslaught. He had not bothered to take aim—merely firing and reloading as quickly as possible—but he was astonished to see the British soldiers falling, nevertheless. In later years, when he thought about it, he concluded that the Kentucky rifle had been far more accurate than the smoothbore muskets he had learned to use as a child.

Now, as he stood at the railing of the sternwheel riverboat, he realized that once again he was approaching Chalmette plantation. Across the river, on what was known locally as the west bank (although it was, due to the curious geography of the alluvial delta, more south and east than west), Jackson and his Americans had placed artillery batteries.

"That's where it happened, is it not?" Randolph said. No need to specify what "that" was.

"That's it."

"It's hard to imagine, seeing it now after all these years, how a battle could have occurred there," Randolph said. "There's hardly a sign of it today."

"I know," Beede said. "I was thinking the same. But it happened, all the same. Seth and I weren't even supposed to be there. We were sutlers, not soldiers."

"I have often wished that I could have been there," Randolph said. "Many free colored volunteers participated, I know. We slaves were not encouraged to join the battle, however."

"You were barely five years old."

"I believe so. I was new to New Orleans in that day. If anyone knew my true age, it would have been my mother."

"You were rather young for fighting redcoats."

"Perhaps," Randolph said. "I was not, however, thought to be too young for picking cotton. I was in the fields every day until I was purchased by M'sieur Dumond."

"I understand the British offered freedom to any slaves who escaped and came over to their side," Beede said.

"So I heard, also. If circumstances had been different, and if any of my slave comrades had chosen to defect, I might well have done so. In view of the outcome of events, we were fortunate not to have succumbed to the temptation."

The plains—swamps, rather—of Chalmette receded into the background. Ahead of them stretched the river. They were making good time, going with the inexorable downstream current.

Turnips, Louisa decided, had never tasted so good. And fatback pork, and hominy, and something hot and sweet that might have been—she wasn't sure, never having tasted it before—coffee. She hoped that Tansy was not bringing trouble on herself by serving such a generous repast to a mere slave, and an escaped slave, at that.

Louisa thought these things but said nothing. She was far too busy shoveling food into her mouth as quickly as she could. Once, an involuntary moan of pleasure escaped her lips, and Tansy laughed.

"Been a long time since you ate, I reckon. Ain't nothin' better than a full belly."

"You reckoned right. Lord, I ain't ate like this in a long time."

"Don't overdo it, now," Tansy said. "You got a long way to go yet today. You can't stay here too long. It ain't safe."

"I ain't got noplace to go," Louisa said, realizing with a sinking feeling that she spoke the truth. She knew no one nearby with whom she could take refuge. She did not even know where she was.

"Don't you worry about that," Tansy said. "I'se makin' arrangements."

Chapter 11

"The place you're lookin' for is up around that next bend," said the deckhand, pointing a gnarled index finger at a point off the left side of the bow.

The plantation house was hidden in a grove of cypress about a hundred yards from the riverbank, the house's roof only glimpsed through the leaf cover. Beede could see no signs of life.

"It appears to be deserted," he said.

"It probably ain't, though. They probably out in the fields. Won't be nothin' but house slaves up there, middle of the day like it is."

That sounded plausible. Beede and Randolph moved toward the bow to see the house as soon as it came into view.

It was a yellowed wood-frame house, dappled in shadow from the spreading live oaks that surrounded it.

Beede had a sense of quiet and peace surrounding it, although he wondered whether the impression was accurate. In his experience, limited as it was, such enforced communities often hid deep passions and bitter hostilities. Even in his own small New England community, antagonism and resentment often appeared, uninvited, at every social gathering—and there were no slaves in New England.

He glanced at Randolph, who stood beside him at the railing, nervously licking his lips in anticipation. No doubt the imminent meeting of fantasy and reality was causing concern.

"The end of your quest is at hand," Beede said, quashing his doubts for the moment.

"Yes, of course," Randolph said. He had, apparently, had second thoughts as well and was tempering his enthusiasm.

The boat was drifting toward the jetty now, and the stern paddlewheel began churning in reverse to slow its approach. Randolph was first to step ashore.

"It is almost as if the plantation has been abandoned," he said.

"It *is* quiet," Beede said.

"More than quiet. Lifeless. There are no cooking smells. No smoke from the kitchen, nor from the big house. There are no children running helter-skelter."

"True," Beede said. "I find it quite strange."

"I find it disturbing," Randolph said. "There are few Indians here anymore. Otherwise I would think this was the remains of an Indian massacre. Something has happened."

The house was neither new nor particularly well kept, Beede saw. It was a large clapboard affair with an exterior veranda that ran the length of the structure and that appeared to sag toward one end. The wood thirsted for paint. It had been painted white, in the American manner, but he could see the yellow-ocher Creole color showing through beneath it. What paint there was had blistered badly in the humid summers, and red roof shingles lay randomly around the grounds where the wind had deposited them. Southern Louisiana was notoriously hard on buildings, and maintenance was a constant problem. In this case, the problem had gotten out of hand sometime past.

Beede knocked at the front door. No response was forthcoming. He was about to knock again, louder, but he was stopped by a man's voice. The man was approaching the house from the way Beede and Randolph had come.

"You gents lookin' for somethin'?"

He was a white man in his early forties, Beede guessed, tall and sandy-haired, and cursed with a red, bulbous nose that sat oddly amid the otherwise regular features of his face. He strolled slowly toward them, frock coat slung over his right shoulder, wide-brimmed hat in his left hand.

Beede stepped toward him, extending his hand

"Good morning," he said. "I am Josiah Beede, and this is my friend Randolph. We are here in the hope of speaking with Mrs. Esther Hawkins."

The man nodded, ignoring Beede's hand. "Pleased. Your friend Randolph have a last name?"

"Not at present," Randolph said. "I have not yet decided."

"Freed man, huh?" the man said. "Prob'ly be good to

get a last name sometime so people don't get the idea you're a slave."

"Yes, I agree. I've not had the time—or the need—till now."

"And you are . . ." Beede said, prompting.

"Right," said the man. "Sorry. Conrad Schneider. I'm the sheriff here. Mind tellin' me why you wanted to see Miz Hawkins?"

"I'm sorry," Beede said. "That's a matter to be discussed with Mrs. Hawkins personally."

"Well, now, that'll be a mite difficult," Schneider said. "Seein' as how she was murdered not long ago, she ain't in any condition to be receivin' visitors."

"Murdered!" Randolph said.

"Coupla days ago. Ain't no doubt about it. We took her body away with a bullet in her chest. So I think you owe me an explanation of how you got here so soon after, and why you're here in the first place."

"Yes, of course. It's a rather simple story, really . . ."

"Hold on just a minute," Schneider said. "Ain't no reason why we have to stand around outside like a flock of buzzards. Not while I got a key to the house."

They sat in the receiving room on the first floor, and Beede and Randolph alternately explained their mission. Schneider listened without comment or reaction until they had finished.

"None of the slaves are here," he said, finally. "They'll probably be sold, but it ain't happened yet. We couldn't leave 'em here, though, with the mistress dead and the overseer missin'. We made other arrangements."

"Where'd they go?"

"Farmed 'em out to other plantations, most 'em," Schneider said. "There's a couple of 'em nobody wanted, so I locked them up in the jail in town. And Howie, my deputy, took one. He's been wantin' a slave for some little time now, to help him in his black-smithin' business. Miz Hawkins had one boy with some experience in that line, so Howie took him on."

"The one we're looking for is a woman," Beede said. "A young woman, perhaps twenty-five or so, named Louisa. Most likely she was a cook. Where could we find her?"

"Well, sir, that's a good question. I'd like to know the answer to that one myself. Her and that overseer both took off about the time Miz Hawkins was shot, and we ain't seen hide nor hair of either one of them. Sure would like to, though."

"Surely you don't think she was involved in mur-der," Beede said.

"Don't know what to think," Schneider said. "She and the overseer both gone missin', and the old lady dead. A lot of explanations come to mind, and I don't know which one is right. Did they run off together? Did she run off and he went chasin' her? Either of 'em coulda shot the old lady, or they coulda been in it to-gether. That's what I'd like to find out."

"Louisa could not have committed murder," Ran-dolph said. "It is not in her nature."

Schneider looked at him for the first time. "Know her, do you?"

"She's my wife."

The sheriff considered this. "Well, I was married once, but I couldn't say for certain that she'd never kill anybody. There was a time when either one of us might have killed the other one without even a second thought. Turns out she went first, or I might be sittin' in my own jail by now, waitin' for the hangman."

"I know my wife, sir."

"Oh, I'm sure you do," Schneider said. "The thing is, you ain't seen her for a while, I figger, or you wouldn't have to be lookin' for her now. A lot of things can happen over time, specially to a slave, whose life ain't under her own control. Maybe you don't know everything that's happened to her since the last time you saw her."

"You say the old lady was shot?" Beede asked.

"A single shot to the chest, clean as a whistle. With a pistol, looks like. There was a old duelin' pistol lyin' on the floor not far away."

"Where'd a slave get a dueling pistol?"

"Hell, where'd *anybody* get a duelin' pistol? Most folks wouldn't see the need, I don't think. Esther Hawkins was sixty if she was a day, and her husband has been dead ten years or more. If it was hers, why'd she keep it? Women don't fight duels."

"The overseer?"

"Well, I considered that, but it don't make much sense, either. Who'd fight a duel with an overseer? Who'd consider him an equal? No, I think the gun most likely belonged to the old lady, probably was her husband's."

"And she knew how to load it, and fire it?" Beede asked.

"Now, there's another conundrum, ain't it? I didn't know the lady, so I can't say for certain, but it don't seem likely that she'd have had cause to know how to use it. Can't see her takin' it out for target practice."

"Any possibility she killed herself?" Beede asked.

"Don't see how she could of killed herself and then disposed of the gun and thrown the other'n halfway across the room. Granted, it's a small room, but it ain't that small. And considerin' she was shot in the chest, I don't think she woulda been able to throw anything after that. I think the killer probl'y took it with him. Or her."

"So you assume that she was killed by the girl, Louisa," Beede said.

"No, sir, I don't," said Schneider. "I don't have enough evidence to assume anything about anybody. But she sure does look good for it, I'd say."

"What about the overseer?" Randolph asked.

The sheriff nodded. "Him, too, of course, although it seems to me her motive's a lot stronger. But I can't rule out the overseer. For that matter, I can't rule out a conspiracy of the two of them."

Beede thought. One person dead, two people missing, and a murder weapon left in plain sight. Something did not add up.

"I'd like to see the room where this happened," he said.

The sheriff shrugged. "Can't see any harm in that. Come on, and I'll show you."

They accompanied Schneider upstairs. The room was smaller than Beede had expected, more like a servant's quarters than the chamber of a plantation mistress. Although it was equipped with the usual accoutrements—a pitcher and basin, a chamber pot nestled in the corner, a small dresser, a ladder-back chair—

it was the bed that dominated the room. Beede pictured the woman lying face up on the yellow spread, eyes vacant, a round hole staring obscenely at those who were unfortunate enough to find her.

"And the gun?" he said.

"It was on the floor just under the window," Schneider said. "I got it now, of course, at my office."

"And it had been fired?"

"No, sir. Weren't even loaded, but if it had been, it would have made the kind of hole we found in the old lady. Funny thing is, it was all alone. Dueling pistols come in pairs, you know. Haven't found the other one."

"Strange," Beede said.

"I thought so. Did the killer bring it with him? Hard to believe. Even if he came plannin' to kill the old lady, he coulda found all sorts of weapons right here in the house. A fireplace poker, for instance."

"And no one has seen the girl?"

"Neither the girl nor the overseer," Schneider said. "We scoured the swamp around here and didn't find hide nor hair of either one. Of course, there's places out there that we can't get to without a boat—a pirogue or somethin' like it. The water ain't too deep, most places, but there's an awful lot of it."

Behind the house was the kitchen. Beede saw the signs of habitation there, but he could not ascertain how long it had been since its occupant had left. Randolph believed that he saw signs that the occupant had been Louisa—*his* Louisa—but he could not be certain.

"I gave her this," he said, holding up a wooden talisman that he had found while rummaging through the pallet on the kitchen house floor. It was a small, human-like figure that Beede thought resembled a *gris gris,* the

sort of totem that practitioners of voodoo often gave—
or sold—to their supplicants

"Are you certain?" Beede asked.

"I believe so," Randolph said. "But no, I can't be
certain. It looks like the one I gave her, but many of
these devices look alike. Still, it has raised my hopes,
which were sagging once more."

"But why would it have been left behind? Why did
she not take it with her?" Beede asked.

"Maybe she had to leave in a hurry," Schneider said.
"If you've just killed somebody, chances are you
wouldn't wait around to search for your possessions."

"Can you take us to the overseer's cabin now?"
Beede asked.

"Might as well," said Schneider. "You've seen most
everythin' else."

The darkness was so profound that they seemed to
be entering a bottomless chasm. They walked without lights to guide them. Tansy had been firm about
that; lights might give them away. The slave patrols had
been looking for Jasper for months, and it would not be
helpful for a potential guest to lead them to their quarry.

Louisa stumbled on a root and fell forward onto her
guide. Tansy, fortunately, was firmly planted and did
not budge.

"Careful about them roots," she said. "They ain't
easy to see in the dark so you gots to keep an eye out."

"Will we see 'gators out here?" Louisa asked. "I
heard stories about them. Don't think I want to meet up
with one."

Tansy laughed. "Don't worry about them," she said.

"We ain't likely to see a 'gator in December. And iffn we do, that ol' 'gator's gon' be real sleepy."

Louisa wasn't certain she was reassured by that, but she decided not to think about it.

"Who is it we going to see?"

"He's a slave, like you and me only he done run off from his plantation, and he be livin' out here for a while. The slave catchers don't come back here much, unless they gots somebody to lead them."

"Would somebody do that?"

"Most folks wouldn't. Another slave might, if it was worth his while. If they catch him and offer him his freedom if he leads them to Jasper's hiding place, maybe."

"Does a lot of people know his hiding place?"

"Only slaves, honey. Only slaves."

She did not realized they had entered the clearing until she found herself looking up at a sky full of stars—stars that had been impossible to see only a few seconds before, due to the overhanging foliage. Her eyes were not yet sufficiently adjusted to the blackness all around her, but she could sense the presence of human forms nearby. She was seized by an unfathomable fear.

"Where we at?" Her voice was a croak.

"We where we planned to be," Tansy whispered. "Now hush a little. When they want you to talk, they ax you."

"Who?"

"You'll see directly. Jes' wait quiet."

One of the dimly perceived shadows detached itself from the curtain of black and moved slowly toward them.

"Tansy? That you?"

"Hey, Jasper. How you doin'?"

The apparition took on human form. "We doin' all right jes' now," the specter said softly. "Had us a good scare night before yesterday, but we managed to get away. One of my boys got caught out on the road by one a' them patrols. Thought we might have to kill somebody, for a while. They never seen the rest of us, though, so everybody else safe."

"Too bad."

"Yeah, well, wouldna happened if Robert had the sense of a chicken. Had a hankerin' for some pork and went to boost a pig and couldn't wait for sundown before makin' his move. By the time I gits there, them pattyrollers are out lookin' for him, and it's all I could do to git my boys under cover."

He was close enough now that Louisa could see a tall, rangy man whose color was nearly as light as her own. He had thick, wavy, reddish hair, a generous hawk beak of a nose, and long arms capped with enormous hands. He walked in a sort of hunch, as tall men sometimes do, so that his head seemed to arrive long before the remainder of his body.

Jasper, in turn, was studying her. He had a way of looking that chilled her to the bone, like a hawk studying its prey. She wanted to look away but did not dare to do so.

"Jasper, this is Louisa," Tansy said. "I told her you could maybe help her. She needs a place to hide for a spell."

"I 'spect somethin' can be worked out," he said, inspecting her rather more closely than she would have preferred. "You the girl from over there at Twin Oaks? What killed ol' lady Hawkins?"

"I didn't kill nobody!" Louisa said, feeling her face grow hot. "I didn't even know she was dead till Tansy told me today."

Jasper shrugged.

"Don't make me no never mind," he said. "They's some folks just *need* to be killed. Sounds like she was maybe one of them. Anyway, we can put you up for a little while, hide you from the white folks, maybe help you get away a little later. You just come along with me, and we'll take care of you."

He grasped her firmly just above her elbow. Louisa, panicked by the sudden movement, glanced fearfully at Tansy.

"Jasper, you let go of her! You gon' scare her half to death grabbin' her like that. She'll go along with you if you don't scare her."

To Louisa's surprise, Jasper let go of her arm. "You right, Tansy," he said. "I just gets antsy out here in the clearin' like this. Too easy to be spotted here. We need to get outta here and back in the woods."

He made for the edge of the clearing, then turned to Louisa.

"You comin'?"

"You go on along with Jasper," Tansy said. "He'll take good care of you, 'cause if he don't, he knows I gon' feed him to the 'gators."

"She would, too," Jasper said, laughing. "She is one tough bird."

He started off toward the edge of the clearing, again, and Louisa followed a step behind.

"Mind you," Jasper said, "if you was to give me some of that money, I'd be real grateful."

"What money?"

"Why, the money you took when you killed ol' lady Hawkins. I heard she had buried treasure hidden in that old house of hers. I hear it ain't there anymore."

"I didn't kill her!" Louisa said. "I told you that already!"

"So you did," Jasper said. "Guess I just forgot."

Chapter 12

The overseer's cabin told them nothing they hadn't known before. It was a single room with a single door, a single window, and a single bed. Both the door and the window had been placed in such a way that they would have provided almost no light for most of the day. There was a dirt floor.

"Has the room been stripped?" Beede asked.

"It is just as we found it," Schneider said.

"No personal possessions? A Bible? A bottle?"

"Nothing. Like as not, he took it all with him when he lit out."

"Then he must have left of his own volition and wasn't planning to return," Beede said. "Any indication which way he went?"

"Not even footprints. Normally we get so much rain around here that the ground is soft, permanent-like. But it's been a couple weeks since we've had a drop. We even looked for signs of a footpath through the underbrush, but we didn't find none."

"Could he have gone by river?"

Schneider leaned out the door of the cabin and spat prodigiously on the ground. "Sure. That's the way most folks go around here. There's even a riverboat or two overnight. It'd be hard to flag 'em down at night, though, without a torch or somethin'. That would attract attention."

"And a riverboat landing in the middle of the night would attract attention, too." Beede said. "Perhaps a small boat?"

"Stayin' close to the bank and out of the main channel where the steamboats go? I suppose he might've gone that way. But it would be real slow goin', in the dark, without a torch or somethin'. And he'd have to go downstream. He'd wear himself out paddlin' against the current."

"How might he have gone, if not by the river?"

"Through the swamp," Randolph said. "The usual escape route for slaves is through the swamps, where the dogs will have trouble following."

"Travis ain't a slave, though," Schneider said.

"Louisa is," Randolph pointed out. "If they left together, they would have gone that way. And if they *didn't* leave together, Travis might well have followed her."

"Good point," Schneider said thoughtfully. "And if Travis followed, we might as well follow, too."

"No," said Randolph. "*I* will follow."

"Don't be a fool," Beede said. "What if you're captured?"

"I have my papers," Randolph said. "They prove that I'm nobody's slave."

"Papers won't make much difference if the slave patrollers catch you," Schneider said. "You wouldn't be the first colored man whose papers got burned up, accidental-like."

"Then I shall have to avoid the patrols, mustn't I? I was a slave, once, on a plantation much like this one. I know the way of things. I believe that I can do it."

"I cannot let you do this," Beede said. "If you are captured, I may not be able to save you."

"With respect, sir, I am no longer your slave, and you have no right to stop me. I am a free man, seeking my wife. This is my right and my duty."

"A damn risky duty, if you don't mind my sayin' so," Schneider said. "I sympathize with your aspiration, but don't you think you'd be better off goin' with a group? Safety in numbers and all?"

"No, sir, I do not. As a colored man, I will be able to go to places where you would not be welcome, places that you in fact do not even know exist. No colored man—no slave, at least—would dare to answer the questions I will ask if a white man accompanied me. Far from ensuring my safety, your presence would put me in great peril."

The white men digested this in silence.

"I hate to say it," Schneider said, finally, "but you make considerable sense."

"I don't like it," Beede said.

"You are not required either to like it or to approve of it," Randolph said. "The moment you turn your back, I can disappear into the swamp. You would not see me again until I chose to make myself visible to you. I can find refuge here; you cannot."

"The boy's right, you know," Schneider put in.

"I came with you to Louisiana because it was not safe for you to go alone," Beede said in protest. "Now I'm told that my assistance is not wanted, or needed. I find it difficult to understand."

"Your assistance, sir, has already been invaluable," Randolph said. "Nevertheless, just as there are places that I may not go, there are places that *you* may not go. Believe me when I tell you that I would prefer to avoid these places myself; I am not unaware of the danger. And yet, I feel that I must do so if I am to find my wife."

"Then let us organize a search party," Beede said. "A group of people can cover more ground than can a single man working alone."

"A search party of white men, you mean," Randolph said. "I would not put my wife in such peril. No, there's nothing for it but that I must go alone."

Beede and Schneider were silent, considering this.

"Well," said Schneider, eventually, "if you're determined to go, I don't guess we can stop you. But let's at least make some plans in case things turn sour."

"Ladies and gentlemen," Jasper said, "we gots ourselves a guest. Her name's Louisa."

He beckoned her to his side, where she stood reluctantly for the little knot of people to inspect her. She was reminded of the days she had spent at the slave market. This time, at least, no one poked and prodded, scrutinizing her teeth, her mouth, her breasts.

"She can sleep with me. I can find room for her."

The speaker was a large, muscular fellow whose
close-cropped hair melded imperceptibly into sideburns
and thence into a close-cropped beard. The remark,
which apparently echoed the sentiments of a number of
the men present, brought forth rumblings of laughter
from around the circle. Louisa shivered involuntarily.

"Now, we ain't gonna have none of that," Jasper
said. "I tole you, she's our guest, an' we gone treat her
nice."

"Oh, I'll treat her nice," the speaker said. "Don't
need to worry none about that. I'll treat her *real* nice.
She'll enjoy it."

Louisa wondered if she had blundered in over her
head. Was she to be handed around among the men like
a jug of whiskey? If so, she might well have placed herself in more danger by attempting to escape than she
had imagined. At this point Jasper was defending her,
but she knew that it might not last. A man like that lived
by playing the odds. If, at some point, she became dis-
posable to him, she had no doubts that Jasper would ac-
cede to his band's desires and consign her to the lust of
the mob.

She glanced around her, seeking possible escape
routes, if one were required. There were maybe thirty
people present, mostly men. They would be a formida-
ble obstacle if she attempted to escape. In truth, she had
not the least idea where she might be, so even if she succeeded in avoiding the circle of her fellow fugitives, she
would be at a loss to find her way—and she would, most
likely, be in even greater danger if she succeeded.

"I tol' you we ain't gettin' into this," Jasper said,
raising a hand to quiet the audience. "I promised Tansy,

over to the Craighead place, that we'd treat this little girl right, and we gon' do just that."

"*I* didn't promise Tansy *nothin'*," the speaker said. "I don't make damn fool promises like that. What's the matter with askin' this pretty little thing to put out a little, in payment, like, for our ass-sistance?"

"It ain't gon' happen, Robert," Jasper said. "Jist forgit it."

"Who's gon' guarantee that you don't take her yerself?"

"I will."

The throng parted, and a woman appeared before them. She was tall and slim, with a long, angular face. She stood next to Louisa and addressed the crowd.

"Jasper's right," she said. "Y'all forgit . . . we's all wanted by the white folks ourselves. Onliest way we can keep ourselves safe is by keepin' faith with them as helps us. Tansy's been real good to us, and we owe her a lot. I'm gonna keep this little girl safe, like Jasper promised."

"Why does Jasper get to make the promises?"

"Because," said the woman, "Jasper's still got the brains God gave him, and you, Robert, is so dumb you nearly gits yourself caught over a pig."

The crowd laughed appreciatively, and the laughter was sprinkled with hoots of derision aimed at Robert.

"You sure tole him, Lucy!" another woman shouted, and Louisa felt some slight relief at this apparent turn of events.

"Another reason," Lucy said. "If you go agin' me, I might decide not to cook for you anymore. You'd have to do for yourself."

More laughter. Louisa glanced at Robert, afraid to

make eye contact but anxious to see how he was taking the ridicule being dished out so generously.

What she saw made her heart sink: Robert stood rigid, balled fists held stiffly at his side, lips compressed in a tight line. His eyes were moving, however, and the glare he fastened on her was hot enough to ignite kindling.

Apparently Lucy saw the look, also, for she put her arm around Louisa's shoulders and whispered in her ear.

"Don't you worry about ol' Robert, honey," she said. "He's mostly talk."

The use of the word "mostly" did not, Louisa felt, inspire confidence.

Chapter 13

Beede and Randolph agreed to meet again in five days at the plantation big house. After that, Schneider suggested, Randolph should forget about returning to the plantation and endeavor, instead, to get a message to him. Schneider would, in turn, get a message to Beede.

"You'll want to follow the river, much as you can," Schneider said. "The big plantations all got riverfront landings so they can git their sugar and cotton to market."

"I don't think they'll be seeking a plantation," Randolph said. "They're fugitives, after all. People will be searching for them there. I'll take to the bayous, I think."

"That maybe makes good sense," Schneider said. "But watch yourself careful out there."

"I shall," Randolph said. With no further preliminaries, he turned and walked to the edge of the woods and vanished onto a pathway that Beede had not noticed.

"I didn't even see that path," Schneider said. "Maybe he'll do okay out there, in spite of us."

"I wish I felt better about this," Beede said.

"I know what you mean, Mr. Beede. Ain't nothin' we can do about it now, though. In the meantime, whyn't you come on home with me? I'll have Miz Richard rustle somethin' up for supper. These Frenchies don't know much about much of anythin' else, but they sure know how to find good cooks."

"It would be my pleasure," Beede said.

Randolph began to regret his haste almost immediately. It was one thing to strike out on his own in familiar territory, though even that would be difficult in the dark. It was quite another to venture into unknown territory in total darkness. It had not been quite dusk when he had left the others, but in the woods it was infinitely darker than it had been in the clearing, and what light there was was dimming quickly.

The path, at least, was well marked and, so far, easy enough to follow. Most likely it was one of those trails that slaves used when making their nighttime visits from plantation to plantation—visiting parents, or wives who lived elsewhere. Such visits were not encouraged by slave owners but were not strictly forbidden, either. That explained why the path was not hidden with greater subtlety.

But for that reason it was not the path that a fugitive would take, and Louisa was a fugitive. There would be another trail, probably branching off from this one, and he would have to look carefully to find it.

As fate would have it, he nearly overlooked it. It was covered with underbrush, and he would have missed it had he not brushed against some foliage and noticed that it gave way at his touch. Quickly he moved it aside, exposing a narrow trail barely large enough for a single person to walk

It might, or might not, be the way she had gone; indeed, if she had not had assistance, he felt certain that she would not have found this passage.

But he had assumed all along that she *had* received help—and perhaps was still receiving help—in her flight. That was what slaves did, help each other. It was important to do so in ways that would not expose the rescuer to danger, but that was not difficult, most of the time. And every slave knew that the day might well come when he himself needed assistance; all the more reason to provide it for others, when he could.

Another thought came to him, however, and it sent a chill through him. Did she run away with Travis, the overseer? And if so, would she now prefer that man to him? He had not considered that possibility until this moment.

And yet another sobering thought: Did she kill Esther Hawkins, her slave mistress? He had assumed that she had not, but what was the basis for his assumption? He had not seen her for four years. He could not know what might have happened to her in that time.

But did it matter? Would he feel differently about her if she had murdered the old lady?

He thought about it for several minutes, even pausing on the pathway to concentrate on the question.

No, he concluded. If her guilt or innocence made any difference, it was only that a guilty woman could not legally be taken out of Louisiana. It would be necessary to smuggle her in some fashion. He abhorred murder and those who resorted to it, but in the bedrock of his soul he abhorred slavery more. If murder was required to free Louisa from slavery, then so be it.

He resumed walking, pushing aside the pangs of conscience. The important thing—the *only* important thing, he told himself—was to find her. Everything else was for another day.

Schneider boarded with a Creole family about a mile from the Hawkins plantation. In deference to Beede, and the fact that he had no mount, Schneider had offered his own black-and-white gelding. Beede had declined the offer, so both men walked while Schneider led his horse by the halter.

"You know what I don't understand, Mr. Beede?" Schneider said as they walked. "These folks I'm livin' with don't have but a coupla hundred acres of land. You can't do much down here with two hundred acres. They raise a few crops, they have a kitchen garden, and a few hogs and chickens. Old man Richard could manage this place on his own, especially with the help of his two strappin' sons, and maybe even clear a small profit. But he's always livin' hand to mouth because he's feedin' two slaves as well as his family."

"That's rather common down here," Beede said.

"So I gather," Schneider said. "But here's what I don't understand: If you *could* make a decent living without slaves, why would you keep one? Why take on that extra expense?"

"Prestige," Beede said.

"Prestige?"

"They call it honor. Down here, your position in society is determined by your possessions. Big house, lots of land, slaves . . . they're all part of what makes you an important man among your peers."

"But if it puts you in debt—"

"They're all in debt," Beede said. "It's the way they live."

"I find that difficult to believe," Schneider said. "I travel a bit around the parish in my position. Some of these planters own thousands of acres, and their harvests are worth several thousand dollars a year. And their houses, some of them, are like palaces. How can they be in debt?"

"Borrowing is a way of life here," Beede said. "This year's crop is already mortgaged to pay for next year's planting. Their houses are money pits, always needing repairs, and they're always enlarging their houses, buying seed, acquiring their neighbors' land, buying slaves they don't even need."

"I've seen that," Schneider said. "But I don't understand the why of it."

"Appearance," Beede said. "Appearance is all. Holding and managing slaves is one of the ways a man demonstrates his importance and makes an impression on his peers."

"Even if you can't afford 'em?"

"Even then."

"Well, I surely don't understand it," Schneider said.

"What happens if one of these planter fellows goes broke? Wouldn't he be exposed as a charlatan?"

"Perhaps. But the onus would fall also on the man who exposed him. That would be considered a dishonorable act."

"That's a funny idea of honor."

"I'd have thought so, also," Beede said. "Nevertheless, I have discovered that this is the way of things in the slave states." And, in saying so, Beede realized that this was one of the reasons why he had not been able to continue living in the South, even as a young man married to a young southern woman. He had not wished to believe it, but he knew that the death of Adrienne, his young wife, had been fortunate—for him, at least. During their marriage they had grown farther apart until, at the end, they had little to say to each other. He had become increasingly uncomfortable in the South, and she had grown increasingly distressed in Washington City, where they had moved after Jackson's election to the presidency. In a few more years they would have existed in a chilly silence that would have been painful to them both.

Schneider shook his head. "I'll never understand these people," he said. Beede silently agreed, though he did not say so.

They came upon a ramshackle building constructed in the Creole manner, on a platform of stilts that raised the living quarters high enough to catch the fleeting breeze. Like many other such houses, it was in desperate need of paint and window glass, and two of the supporting stilts appeared to be rotting away in plain sight.

"This is where I'm living," Schneider said in a low

voice. "Not somethin' I woulda chose myself, but I ain't got the money to be choosy."

Surprisingly, the interior of the house was remarkably well kept. The wide board floors had been swept and scoured, and an attempt—albeit unsuccessful—had been made to reclaim a finish to the rudimentary furniture.

"Miz Richard does her best," Schneider said. "But she ain't got much to work with."

"I see."

They stood in the main room a minute, each apparently lost in his thoughts.

"Well," said Schneider. "I'm starved. Let's see what Miz R can rustle up for us to eat."

As it happened, supper consisted of many of the foods he had yearned for during his years away from Louisiana. Oysters and rice, two great delicacies reserved for special occasions in New England—if they were served at all—were mainstays of the diet in Louisiana, even at poor tables such as this. They were prepared simply and without pretense, but Beede caught himself consuming shameful quantities before he remembered to exercise restraint. After all, he reminded himself, while these foodstuffs were treats to him, they were sustenance to his hosts. He extended heartfelt praise to Madame Richard and was rewarded with a very becoming blush and a beam of pleasure from her husband, old August Richard.

Afterward, Beede and Schneider sat by the fire with their pipes, joined by Richard, whose English was far better than Beede's rusty French.

"It was necessary to become fluent in the language," Richard said in explanation, "for the Americans have

quite overrun us. I fear it will soon become very difficult to engage in commercial transactions in any other
language."

"Just as well," said Schneider with the trace of a
grin. "French is abominably difficult if you want to actually *say* somethin'. It sounds great when you're
talkin' with your mouth full, but it ain't much good for
anythin' else, I don't think."

"It is a beautiful language," Richard protested hotly,
rising to the bait. "It is the language of a great civiliza-
tion, and it has withstood the test of time."

"Well, let's be honest, here, August," Schneider said.
"You Frenchies never had to talk to anybody much
about anythin' important. Aside from *'voulez-vous'* and
'mais oui,' Frenchies never have much to say." He
caught Beede's eye and winked.

"Two very important concepts," Richard said, catch-
ing the spirit of the thing. "Will you?' and 'yes.' Where
would you be today if your father had not said 'Will
you?' and your mother had not said 'yes'?"

"A telling point, m'sieur," agreed Schneider, with a
laugh. "An excellent point, indeed. But Mr. Beede and
I are eager to discuss another matter with you, if you
will oblige us. What can you tell us about ol' Miz
Hawkins, your late neighbor?"

"I can tell you little," Richard said. "Except that she
was not French."

"American?"

"I believe, perhaps, Scottish."

"Well, that's very interesting, August," Schneider
said. "What makes you say that?"

"It is *très simple,* m'sieur. Her husband was Scottish,

and he sent for her not long after he settled here. I assumed, therefore, that she, too, came from Scotland."

"How long ago was that?"

Richard thought. "Quite some time ago. Perhaps twenty-five years, for M'sieur Hawkins. A year or two later for Madame."

"Interesting," said Schneider. "That would have been about the time of that big fracas outside of New Orleans, wouldn't it? A Scotchman wouldn't have been real popular around here back then."

"Was M'sieur Hawkins perhaps a military man?" Beede asked. "I remember a friend of mine saying recently that a contingent of Scottish Highlanders was nearly annihilated during the British attack. In the heat of battle, it would be easy for a deserter to disappear."

"It is possible," Richard said. "He was a big man, very strong, very tall, and he held himself erect, like a soldier. I did not ask his provenance; we were not close."

"If he deserted, he'd not likely have told you, anyway," Schneider said. "Wonder how he came up with the money to buy his land? Not on a soldier's pay, I'll wager."

"I do not know," said Richard. "I know only that he was an indifferent farmer, at best. I believe that he fancied himself a planter and yearned for ever more land and more slaves. More than once he offered to buy my property, slaves and all. Of course, I declined each time, but he was not discouraged."

"The southern disease," Schneider said. "Plantationitis, I call it. The stubborn urge to sit on your veranda sipping a toddy and watch the darkies doin' your work for you. Very seductive, I must say. I could grow accustomed to it myself."

"All the same," said Richard, "there were times when I was tempted to take him up on his offer. I could have taken his money and retired to New Orleans."

"Why didn't you? Sounds like a good plan to me."

"Ah, well," Richard said. "The problem is, it would have left me with nothing to do."

"I could live with that, if the money was right," Schneider said. "I ain't so much enamored of workin' that I couldn't get along without it."

"I am not so fortunate as you," said Richard. "His offers were always more than fair, but I cannot imagine myself existing in idleness. What would I do? I am not so wealthy that I could get myself elected to a public office, and there are few alternatives aside from that."

"I'd think of somethin'," Schneider said. "If I had to. Maybe they'd let me live in one of them whorehouses up in New Orleans. The good Lord knows I could find inspiration all around me if I wanted to spend my life in idleness. A bigger bunch of ne'er-do-wells than this planter class I ain't never seen."

After two hours—or so it seemed to him—Randolph noticed a faint glow of firelight in the night sky. It was still some distance off, and very faint, but there was a nearly imperceptible lightening somewhere ahead. It was far too early for dawn, which would not, in any case, glow quite as yellow as this, or flicker as this did.

It could be a hunting party, he supposed, but he thought not. Whites tended to hunt the easy way, with dogs, and dogs could be heard from miles away. More likely it was a campsite, and a campsite this deep in the woods this late in the winter probably meant runaways.

Louisa might not be with them, of course, whoever they might be. The woods were dense and deep here, and she might not have stumbled on this particular party. However, these runaways might know of her whereabouts, or have seen her, or heard of her. They might even be willing to help him look for her, as long as it did not put themselves in danger. Or perhaps the glow up ahead was the very campsite of Louisa and her overseer.

Moving as quietly as he could, Randolph began closing the distance with the firelight. It was far more difficult to move quietly in the swamp than he had expected, despite the softness of the spongy ground. There were exposed tree roots that caught his foot and caused him to stumble, and soft spots that captured his boots and sucked on them as ardently as leeches. He did not fear snakes or alligators so much in the midwinter darkness—his childhood experience had taught him that they did not venture out much this time of day and year—but he knew that other animals would be less constrained. Cougars, especially, needed to eat all year round and would not be put off by the cold.

He made a number of false steps, for the ground was treacherous. As he approached the firelight, he placed his foot on a root—or so he had thought—that gave way and plunged him up to his thighs in what might have been quicksand.

Feeling the suction pulling him down, he flailed in the darkness until his hands hit on a cypress knee. With great effort, he used the shaggy root as a support and leveraged himself slowly out of his predicament.

On solid ground once again, he brushed off as much of the mud and sand as he could, noting as he did so the growing numbness in his fingers and the stiffening of his trouser legs from the remaining mud. The air was not nearly as cold as winter in New Hampshire, but the ever-present damp nevertheless caused him to shiver uncontrollably. He needed warmth, and quickly, if he hoped to survive the night. The irony of his situation evoked an involuntary smile: to die of the cold in the swamps of Louisiana within sight of his objective, after having survived three freezing, snowclad winters in the foothills of New Hampshire.

Several minutes passed before he realized that the glow in the sky had disappeared.

Had his quarry put out the fire and gone to sleep?

Well, they would have to sleep sometime, without doubt. But both of them? Would not one remain awake to guard against pursuers? They were fugitives, after all. The overseer was a white man, but he could expect no consideration from the slave patrols if he had spirited away a slave under his supervision—especially not a young and attractive and valuable female.

The other possibility was that they had heard his desperate thrashing in the darkness and had doused the fire to confuse him. That seemed more likely. Fortunately, he was close enough now that he no longer needed the firelight to guide his steps. They were less than fifty yards away, if he had calculated correctly.

Cautiously, he crept forward until only a few feet separated him from the campsite. On his hands and knees, he parted the foliage.

A big camp. Much bigger than he had anticipated. He counted ten crude lean-to shelters arranged in a circle, and he thought there might have been more in the darkness behind those he could see. He saw tendrils of smoke wafting to the sky, where the fire had been hastily put out. A few embers still glowed through the ashes under which they had been banked, an indication, he thought, that the fire had been put out rather hastily.

So he *had* been heard. He could think of no other reason for such a precipitous move. He resolved to remain silent and maintain a watch on the village—it was too large to call it a campsite—until the occupants' alarm had passed. Then, when things had grown calmer, he would make his approach, not in a threatening manner but openly, even noisily, to dispel their fears. In the morning, when they could see him clearly, they would be able to see that he meant them no harm and would, perhaps, be willing to give him the assistance he—

He did not complete the thought. He heard a sudden rustling behind him and turned in time to see a tree limb descending to strike him on the temple. He had a fleeting impression of a man wielding the limb as a weapon—a lanky, light-skinned man with improbable reddish hair.

Darkness followed. Darkness and pain.

Chapter 14

"I hope that I am not taking you away from your duties," Beede said the following morning as he and the sheriff set out to visit Schneider's deputy in his blacksmith shop.

"Don't fret yourself none about that," Schneider said. "This *is* my duty. I'm the sheriff, remember. I'm supposed to deal with crimes, and this is the biggest crime we've had around here in a coon's age."

"I suppose murder is a bit out of the ordinary."

"You suppose wrong, then. Murder ain't out of the ordinary, at all. Hell, folks kill each other all the time down here."

"Truly?"

"Truly. Of course, this murder is an *illegal* murder. That's a little different."

"You're confusing me. Is there such a thing as legal murder? What does it consist of?"

"Duels, mostly," Schneider said. "They dress 'em up as affairs of honor, like it was just the gentlemanly way of settling disputes, but mostly they're just plain cold-blooded murders."

"In what way are they murders?"

"Here's the way it works," Schneider said. "Ol' Jacques don't like Étienne and wants him out of the way, so he trumps up some kind of insult and springs it on Étienne. Étienne—like a fool—takes offense and challenges Jacques to a duel. This is what Jacques has been waiting for. He takes up the challenge, which gives him the choice of weapons, and next thing Étienne knows he's lying under an oak tree with a hole in his gut and his blood runnin' out on the ground."

"And honor is satisfied," Beede said.

"Damn right. Honor is satisfied. Of course, Jacques' honor is a little more satisfied than Étienne's, bein' that honor is satisfied more easily from a vertical position."

"I take your meaning," Beede said, amused.

"The problem is, affairs of honor are only for gentlemen. The rest of us have to settle for less respectable types of murder. Knife fights back behind the tavern, slitting throats in an alley, stabbing your wife or your *amour* in the bedroom . . . that sort of thing. It's less honorable but still legal and pretty damn effective for all that."

"You seem to have learned much about the Louisiana way of life," Beede said.

"Well, I got a good teacher. Howie, my deputy we're on our way to see right now, has lived down here all his life. He's been explaining things to me all along so I won't make a fool of myself in the presence of my betters."

"Your betters?"

"If I understand what Howie tells me, near everyone I meet down here is my better, this bein' where God would live if he didn't have to be everywhere at once. I guess I ought to be thankful that these good people let me live among them and throw them in jail now and then when they get drunk."

Schneider had borrowed a horse from a neighbor, so Beede was able to ride the five miles alongside the sheriff. Beede found himself thinking, as he rocked and swayed on the back of the gray nag he had been given the use of, about his own sweet Morgan horse, Peter, awaiting him in New Hampshire. Like most Morgans, Peter was smaller than other breeds, leading the uninitiated observer to conclude that the breed was unsuited to farming. New Englanders had found, however, that the Morgan was stronger than it appeared and far more versatile than an ox.

His mind wandered to thoughts of all he had left behind in New England: his farm, his law practice, his neighbors, the relentless march of the seasons and the chores that inevitably accompanied them—planting, tilling, harvesting, preparing for winter. He thought of the Thanksgiving feast—the highlight of the Yankee year—and the other social occasions that New Englanders found to relieve the loneliness and isolation.

From there, his mind wandered to Deborah Tomkins.

It had been several days since he had thought of her—not since he had last received correspondence from her, in fact. Once she entered his mind, however, he found it difficult to wrench his thoughts away.

What did that mean? It had been that way with Adrienne, those many years ago, but it had been different, also. His infatuation with Adrienne had been a form of intoxication, almost a dream state. When she was with him, an air of euphoria enveloped him, and he wandered in a mist like an absinthe drinker. He had seen them in the taverns of the Old Quarter, staring fixedly with enthralled anticipation at the thick, green liquid as it turned to ocher under the dripping water. He had not been tempted by absinthe; his drug was Adrienne.

Deborah did not affect him in the same manner, but he could not deny that he saw her face often in his mind's eye. He saw not the mystical image of ethereal beauty that Adrienne had inspired. In Deborah he saw honesty, judgment, and acute intelligence cloaked in a serene temperament. But there was passion, too, in her. He had seen how she had reacted to the appearance of the murdered mill girl on his land two years earlier, and he remembered how she had identified with the dead girl and had actually helped him to see where his investigation would need to take him.

Adrienne could not have done that, nor would he have expected her to do so. She certainly would not have identified with an Irish factory girl, nor concerned herself with bringing her murderer to justice. She could hardly read or write and was indifferent to politics, while Deborah maintained a lively interest in current events and the world around her. Beede marveled that two women, so different in nearly every respect, could inspire such similar feelings in his breast.

"Howie's place is right up ahead, here," said Schneider.

•   •   •

Randolph awoke exactly where he had fallen. He lay on his back, and the sun was so bright it hurt his eyes. Moaning, he rolled on his side, facing into the shade. In few moments, when his eyes had adjusted, he sat upright and looked around.

He was alone.

The village of lean-to shelters he had seen the night before—gone. The fire had been doused, and the ashes were cold. Tracks had been brushed over to obliterate any signs of human comings and goings. There were, in fact, few signs that the settlement had ever existed. Clever.

They could not have gone far, he thought. Their portable settlement was designed as a compromise between mobility and comfort. It could be moved, but it was too large to be moved easily. Especially in darkness.

Moving slowly and cautiously because of the throbbing in his head, Randolph stood up and made his way through the brush to the clearing where he had seen the village.

They had taken some pains to disguise their trail, but they also had been in a hurry. He found the trail after a few minutes and set out to follow it with renewed determination.

They had been clever before, more clever than he had suspected. They had fooled him before. They would not, however, do so again.

Chapter 15

Beede heard the clanging of iron on iron before they stepped inside.

"Hey, Howie! You got visitors," Schneider said.

"Mistah Howie ain't here," said the voice inside.

The voice belonged to a barrel-chested man, medium-brown, who paused in his hammering to take in his visitors. The inspection took less than a second before he returned to his work.

"Hello, Sheriff. Mistah Boudreau took off this morning, left me all alone here with this passel of iron to work. Told me I had to git it all done afore sundown."

"Where's he at, then?"

"Don' know, rightly," said the man. "He said he'd be gone mos' of the day."

"So where's *Miz* Howie?"

"All I know is they left together, not long after

breakfast. Missuz was all dressed up like Sunday mornin'. Surprised me, somewhat. First time I see her like dat."

"Mr. Beede," Schneider said in introduction, "this here's George. He's the slave I told you about that worked on the Hawkins plantation. Howie took him on last week. Guess he figured that entitled him to a little vacation."

"Pleased to meet you, George," Beede said. Then, to Schneider: "Think your deputy would mind my asking George a few questions?"

"I don't think he'll know, whether he minds or not," Schneider said. "He won't hear about it from me. Just go ahead and ask him what you want. I'm going to take a little walk around, see what I can see."

Beede waited until Schneider had left before turning back to George.

"I should have asked you if *you* minded, George," he said to the man. "May I ask you a few questions?"

"Long as you don't interrupt me while I'm workin'," George said, lifting the bar he had been hammering and immersing it in water. "And you don't ask me to talk about my masters behind their backs. I'm real par-tick-u-lar about that."

"How about your *former* owner? Mind talking about her?"

"Miz Hawkins? Don't know what I can tell you 'bout her. I was in the fields. Didn't see her much."

"How about Louisa?"

"The cook? Saw even less of her. She hung out in the kitchen pretty much all day long. Didn't seem at all sociable, not like Mary, what was there before."

"Mary was the cook before Louisa?"

"Yassuh. She took sick back last summer and died. Miz Hawkins got Louisa to replace her."

"What happened to Mary?"

"Well, nobody never talked about it much. Don't know that I can tell you for sure."

"What's your guess? You can't hurt Mary anymore by talking about it."

"It ain't Mary I'se worried about," George said.

"You can't hurt Miz Hawkins, either. You know she's dead, too."

"It ain't Miz Hawkins, either."

"Who, then?"

George put down the tongs and leaned close to Beede. "It's that Travis," he said. "That overseer. He can be real mean when he wants to be, and talkin' about Mary is one sure way to set him off."

"Travis has disappeared," Beede said. "I wouldn't be surprised if he turned up dead. In any case, he's gone somewhere, and I doubt he's coming back. I don't think he's a problem."

"That so?" George said. He fished the iron bar from the water again and thrust it into the coals, pumping the bellows with his free hand. "All the same, if he turns up again he could make it mighty hard on ol' George. Don't think I want that."

"He won't know from me," Beede said. "I've never met the man and probably never will."

George considered this. "I got your word on that?"

"You've got my word."

"And you ain't just foolin' a ol' nigger? You means it?"

"I don't trick people."

George removed the bar from the coals and began

hammering it. He continued his work for several minutes, until Beede was ready to conclude the big slave had decided not to answer. Beede continued to wait with as much outward patience as he could manage to display. Eventually George put down his hammer and turned to face him.

"You here lookin' for Louisa, ain't you?"

"Yes."

George nodded. "Figgered so. She's a mighty pretty one, could turn a man's head. And I guess you can't be any worse for her than that Travis is."

"I'm not looking for myself," Beede said. "A friend of mine is married to her, and he wants to buy her freedom."

George shook his head. "I *heard* things are different up north," he said. "Guess it must be true. Ain't many white men gon' marry a nigger girl down here, even one as light-colored as Louisa. He don't need to; all he has to do is take her, if she's a slave like Louisa. And he wouldn't need to set her free, nuther."

"My friend isn't a white man. He's free colored."

"Now, don't that beat all," he said. "That's a fine story. Not that I believes it, o' course, but it don't matter if I believes it. Story like that deserves a story in return."

"So you know where I could find Louisa?"

"Now, I didn't say that, did I? No, I don't know *for sure* where you can find her, but I got a good idea who might."

"Give me the name, and I'll quit bothering you."

"Hold on, now," said George. "I can't do that. What I can do is, I'll get a word to that person tonight, and that person will take a message to the people what's probably got Louisa. Then somebody will get back to you."

"Do we have to be so secretive? I *could* just follow you tonight."

"You *could*," George said. "And you *could* end up lost in the swamp, too. I don't think you want to do that."

"Probably not," Beede said.

"It ain't just probably," George said with a laugh. "I can goddamn guarantee it."

"All right, I'll wait. I'm staying with the sheriff at the Richard place. I guess you'll know how to find me."

"Yassuh."

"You *will* get back to me, now? You won't leave me hanging?"

"Oh, I'll get back to you. It don't do to disappoint a white man down here. I cain't guarantee you'll like the answer, though."

"It's a funny thing," Schneider said as they left the blacksmith shop. "I mean, Howie takin' off like that."

"He had business in town, like as not."

"Maybe," Schneider said. "Man like Howie, though, ain't exactly a mover and shaker, if you know what I mean. He ain't one for high finance or nothin' like that. He ain't got two dimes to rub together, most of the time. Besides, he's supposed to let me know if he leaves town. He's my deputy, after all."

"He'll turn up after a while, and you can ask him."

"I suppose."

Beede noticed, however, that the sheriff wore a troubled air he had not possessed when they had arrived.

"You're worried about something, it appears," Beede said.

"Just tryin' to puzzle somethin' out," Schneider said. "How're you at puzzles?"

"I'll give it a try."

From his pocket, Schneider extracted two five-dollar golden half-eagle coins and handed them to Beede. "What do you make of these?" he asked.

Beede peered closely at the coins. "I haven't seen many of these," he said. "Are they genuine?"

"I don't know. I took them from under George's bedroll."

"You stole them?"

"No, I didn't steal them. They're evidence of something. I don't know what, but I know they're evidence. Besides, I left him a couple of handfuls of dollar coins in their place. He's still got ten dollars; he just ain't got *these* ten dollars."

"Why did you do that?"

"Well, look at it some more. What's your opinion?"

Beede peered at the coins again. "They're rather crude," he said.

"Exactly what I thought. Looks like counterfeit to me. What would a slave be doin' with ten dollars in counterfeit money? Hell, how many slaves have ten dollars in *real* money?

"Maybe George is extra thrifty."

"Even if he is, this is ten dollars we're talkin' about. If a slaveholder gives his people three dollars for Christmas, his neighbors complain that he's spoilin' things for everybody else. If George had been hired out in the city—New Orleans, say—he might salt away ten dollars in a year or two, after expenses. But George came off the Hawkins plantation, and Howie gave me the impression that George has lived his whole life there."

"You're saying he stole them?"

"Maybe. But why would Miz Hawkins have ten dollars lying around so he *could* steal them?"

"I can see why you're concerned."

"Exactly," Schneider said. "And if they're counterfeit, as I suspect, then the whole thing gets really confusing."

"**Y**ou jist don't give up, do you?" said the voice from behind.

Randolph whirled to meet his adversary, knowing full well that he had lost his advantage. The man who faced him was tall, rangy, and of a light complexion— beatable, perhaps, if it were not for the three rather heftier men who accompanied him. Two of the three brandished clubs, and the third held a muzzle-loading gun, which was aimed at his gut.

"I mean you no harm," Randolph said. "I'm looking for someone."

"You a slave?" said the lighter-colored man, who seemed to be the spokesman for the little band. "You don't sound like a slave."

"I once was a slave, but I'm free now."

"Well, so am I," said the coffee-colored man with a laugh. "Long as I stay in the swamp where the pattyrollers skeered to go, I'm as free as any man on earth."

He narrowed his eyes. "So what's you want with us, you free nigger? Want to be a slave again?"

"I'm looking for my wife," Randolph said.

Again, laughter, from all four of them. "Nigger, you sure picked a funny place to go lookin' for a wife," the lighter man said. "This look like a slave market to you?"

"Her name is Louisa."

The laughter ceased.

"Man, I don't know what you up to, but you in the wrong place. Ain't nobody here goes by that name."

No "nigger" this time, Randolph noticed.

"I think you're wrong about that," he said. "But to make sure, let me come in and look. If she's not here, I'll move on."

"Right. You'll move on and tell the white folks where we're hidin' out. You think we stupid?"

"All right," Randolph said. "Let's do it another way. Go back to your camp and talk to her. Tell her my name is Randolph, and I'm here to buy her and bring her home."

The coffee-colored man considered this. Turning to his companions, he said, "I'll go back. Y'all keep an eye on this feller."

Turning back to Randolph, he said, "I'll be back. Don't go 'way, now."

"Don't worry about him, Jasper," said one of the others. "He ain't goin' nowhere. We'll see to that."

Chapter 16

"**R**andolph?"

"Louisa!"

She looked older, Randolph thought, when they broke from their embrace. Of course, she would, as would he, after four years apart. And yet, there were more lines at the corner of her mouth, and in her forehead, than he had expected.

"You look well," she said, holding him at arm's length.

"And you."

"I know how I look," she said. "We have no mirrors here, but I have seen myself reflected in the water of the bayou. Why are you here?"

"You are my wife. I've come to take you back with me."

"To take me where?"

"Home."

"And where is home?" she said with striking bitterness. "I'se a slave, even if you ain't. I cain't go nowhere with you."

"Miz Hawkins is dead; she can have no hold on you now."

"But she got relations, I expects. Guess I belongs to them now. Leastwise, I ain't free."

"You will be. I've been saving up for just this occasion. I plan to buy your freedom and take you back with me to New Hampshire."

"Where's this New Hampshire, and how's we gon' get there? We gon' swim? Or fly like a bird?"

"I don't know," Randolph said, a trace of exasperation creeping into his voice. "Maybe we'll take a steamboat. Or maybe we'll sail down the Mississippi, like we sailed *up* to get here. I'll leave that decision to Mr. Beede. He's traveled much more than I have. He'll know the best way to go."

"Mr. Beede! Is he here with you?"

"He came south with me."

"I don't believe you. Where's he at, then?"

"He should be waiting at the big house, back at Twin Oaks. That's where we parted company."

"And if he ain't?"

Randolph did not answer. It was a question that had concerned him, also.

"I'll figure something," he said eventually.

Five days came and went. Beede procrastinated in the hope that Randolph would return, with or without Louisa. George, the blacksmith slave, never contacted him, despite his promise. After two more days, however, he realized he could no longer impose on August Richard and his family, who had refused to take any payment and yet clearly could not afford to continue hosting him without compensation.

"Sure, if you need to get back to New Orleans, you ought to go," Schneider said. "If your friend turns up, I'll either see to it that he gets back, or I'll get a message to you. I've got your address in the city."

Reluctantly, Beede packed his meager belongings and walked to the river landing to await the steamboat to New Orleans. Schneider accompanied him, and the two passed the time in companionable silence.

"You know, it didn't occur to me until right this minute," Schneider said after a while. "I knew all along that your name was familiar, but I just now realized why that is. Josiah Beede. You're well known around here!"

"I have been to Louisiana before," Beede admitted.

"*Been* here! Hell, you're a hero!"

"I'm not a hero."

"The hell you ain't," said Schneider. "Josiah Beede, the boy hero of New Orleans! You were in Jackson's kitchen cabinet!"

"I worked with President Jackson," Beede said. "And I was at Chalmette during the British invasion. But I was not a hero. I have heard the tall tales, of course, but they are untrue."

"Well," said Schneider with a shrug, "a lot of them tall tales *ain't* true, but most of them have somethin' sorta true about them. Don't matter, anyway, as long as people *think* they're true. And Ol' Hickory must of thought they were true. He sure relied on your advice, is the way I heard it."

"He likes me and seems to respect me," Beede said. "And I like and respect him."

"I heard something else about you," Schneider said. "I heard you're pretty good at solving crimes. There were a couple of murders and a theft or two up in Washington City that I heard about, and seems to me there was something in New England a couple of years back."

"I've had the misfortune to be in the wrong place at the wrong time."

"Wrong place for you," Schneider said. "But maybe the right place for me. Maybe you could give me a hand with this murder thing."

"I don't think I would be much help. You know the people; I don't."

Schneider thought about this. "Maybe so," he said, "although right now I'm thinkin' I don't really know *anybody* down here."

"However little you know, I'm certain that I know less."

"There's the boat comin'," Schneider said, pointing to a plume of smoke rising from downstream. Beede watched as the plume rounded the bend and became a vessel, stack upon ornate stack like a great floating layer cake. He could hear the wheel striving laboriously against the current as it inched its way to the landing.

"One thing you can do for me, if you're amenable," Schneider was saying. "I'd sure like to know more about these coins."

He reached into his pocket and retrieved the gold

half-eagle coins. Beede took them and slipped them into his green lawyer's bag.

"Recently I met a man who works for the new national mint," he said. "We are not friends, but I will go to see him. Perhaps he will be sufficiently interested in pursuing this mystery that our previous differences will be set aside."

"Good enough for me," said Schneider. "Just write to me if you learn anythin'." He was about to say more when the boat pulled up to the landing, and he ran to secure the line thrown to him by a dockhand.

Back to New Orleans. Beede gathered his belongings and went on board, wondering as he went if this southern excursion—which seemed to be enduring longer than he had anticipated—would ever end.

Chapter 17

Returning to New Orleans was more difficult for Beede than he had anticipated. He told himself that he and Randolph had not failed in their quest—they merely had not yet succeeded—but failure was in his heart. Every day that passed—indeed, every hour—might be taking Randolph and Louisa farther apart. Further, every delay in achieving their objective increased the danger to Randolph.

Louisa was, in some sense, safer than Randolph. Whatever else she may be—murderer, runaway, thief—she was also property, and valuable property at that. People would take care with her; she was walking money. Randolph was a free man and thus worth nothing—or next to nothing. If he were taken and sold into slavery, he might be worth more on the market than Louisa, but there were criminal penalties for kidnapping freedmen and returning them to bondage. They were rarely enforced, because of the difficulty in proving that a man was free if a white man said he was not. But Randolph would fight fiercely to avoid being placed under the yoke again.

And he had his papers, which proved his freed status.

The journey upriver took much longer than the trip downstream, which offered Beede many opportunities to berate himself for abandoning his friend and to consider what he must do next to make things right. It seemed clear that even if Randolph succeeded in finding Louisa, she would not be free to go with him unless she were absolved of guilt in the murder of her mistress. Perhaps he could do something toward that end, although guilt was often presumed when masters were killed and slaves were available to be accused of the crime.

What could have been the motive for such a deed? Robbery?

Perhaps. Schneider had said that Esther Hawkins was not a wealthy woman, but she did own land and slaves. It might be useful to determine if she had made a will and, if so, whom she had named as her beneficiary. No doubt, Sheriff Schneider would pursue that avenue; he would have access to the appropriate parish records.

He found a seat alone in the lounge of the riverboat, where he extracted the coins the sheriff had entrusted to him. He had no reason to believe that these coins had any relationship to the murder of Esther Hawkins, but robbery was often the motivation for murder, and they had been found among the possessions of one of her slaves. If there were more of these coins somewhere, perhaps that would be a motive for the old woman's murder.

He studied the coins carefully. They did not display the luster of new coins, but otherwise they had the appearance of gold—and high-quality gold, at that. They felt like gold; their weight was sufficient to be the five-dollar half eagles they professed to be; but neither Liberty on their face nor the eagle on their reverse were as sharply defined as he would expect.

He shook his head, perplexed. It was time to call once again on Monsieur Balfour at the mint, a visit he did not look forward to.

When the boat docked in New Orleans, Beede hired a cab to take him to Pierre Dumond's wineshop, half hoping to find that Randolph had arrived before him, half fearing to learn that Randolph had been captured or killed by slave patrollers. But Pierre reported that he had heard nothing at all.

Beede spent a restless night. He slept little and dreamed much. When awake, he found himself thinking of Randolph, wondering about his fate, worrying that he had been captured, or killed. When he slept, he dreamed of Adrienne, their courtship, their brief marriage, and the look of hate in her eyes as she died of childbirth fever. Toward morning, he discovered that the face on the deathbed had become not Adrienne but Deborah Tomkins. The shock brought him upright in his bed, and he was unable to sleep again, wondering what, if anything, the vision meant.

On the following morning Beede set out for the mint in search of Balfour. He found him in his third-floor office, hunched over a ledger book. A look of irritation flickered on his face before he regained control of his countenance and mustered a brief—and frosty—smile. He rose from his chair but did not offer his hand.

"What may I do for you, sir?"

"I would appreciate your opinion of this," Beede said, handing Balfour the golden half-eagle coins.

"Where did you acquire these?" said Balfour, peering intensely at the coins.

"I would rather not say just now," Beede said. "Are they real?"

"I am uncertain." He turned and placed the coins on a scale that sat on the windowsill behind his desk.

"Interesting," he said.

"What is so interesting?"

"The weight is correct," he said. "Or as near to it as makes no difference. And yet they are not ours. The markings are correct, also, but I do not believe they are true coins of the United States."

"I don't follow you. Do you mean they are worthless?"

"Not at all. I cannot vouch for their true worth with the crude instruments I have at hand, but I would venture to say that they would be accepted most places at their full face value. The assayer would be better able to answer that question."

"Then they are genuine?"

"Ah, well," Balfour said. "It isn't that simple."

"I beg your pardon?"

"Consider for a moment," Balfour said with an expansive gesture, as if settling in for a lecture. "What is it that makes a coin valuable? It is the gold content, is it not? By weighing these coins and comparing their weight to those of the known weight of appropriate gold coins, I can tell you whether a particular piece of metal has sufficient value. I have weighed these coins, and I can assure you that they contain full value."

"Then you're saying they are *not* counterfeit."

"I'm saying nothing of the sort. Indeed, counterfeit is what I believe them to be. But they are counterfeits of a type I have not seen before—counterfeits that possesses full face value."

"How can that be?"

"I confess that I don't understand, myself," Balfour said. "It makes no sense that I can determine. Why would one simulate coins—ones that imitate the real articles so accurately—if not for profit? But if one produces coins that are like the real ones in every respect—including monetary value—what profit can there be? And yet I believe that is what we have here."

"Perhaps they are real after all," Beede said.

"If they are real, they are uncommonly crude," Balfour said. "I don't believe my colleagues in Philadelphia would be satisfied to produce such coins."

Balfour reached into a nearby drawer and extracted a coin that looked, from across the desk, much like the ones in Beede's possession. He set the new coin on its edge and spun it. The coin made a ringing sound as it spun.

"This," said Balfour, "is a genuine half-eagle coin. Now try to spin one of yours."

Beede tried to do so, but the coin would not spin. It began to wobble immediately and quickly fell on its side.

"As you see, your coin is not well balanced," Balfour said. "But more than that, it has a lip around its circumference, which prevents it from standing on end.

Further, it is pitted in a way that a true coin would not be. This is true for both of your coins."

"And that means . . ."

"It means, simply, that these are not legitimate coins of the United States. Amercan coins are struck. This ridge around the edge means that these coins were *not* struck. They were cast!"

"You're saying that someone has created counterfeit coins that approximate the value of legitimate coins," Beede said, the understanding slowly dawning.

"That is correct, sir."

"Can you suggest a reason why someone might have done this?"

"None whatsoever. As I said before, it makes no sense that I can see. What possible monetary gain would accrue to the man who passes these coins? I can see none at all."

"Motive aside, how would it be done? How would one go about duplicating a coin without possessing the dies from which the originals were struck?"

"Lost wax, I presume," Balfour said. "It is a process familiar to sculptors and makers of keys . . . to anyone, in short, who studies the methods of reproducing an object."

"I hesitate to ask this, but please understand that I am not casting aspersions on you or your colleagues. Would it be possible to produce these coins here?"

"Here in the mint, you mean? Certainly it would be possible—but not likely. Coin production is carefully monitored for precisely that reason. Anyone who undertook to produce counterfeit coins here in the mint would probably be discovered rather quickly."

"Then can you suggest other sources for these coins?"

"Certainly. A goldsmith. A silversmith. Any metalsmith, such as a tinsmith. Perhaps a potter. Even a blacksmith could do it. The difficulty is not in duplicating the coins but in obtaining the precious metals from which the coins are made. The question, as I told you, is not how, but why."

"And you cannot imagine why such fakery might be accomplished?"

"I can think of one reason, now that I consider it," Balfour said. "But it seems a bit far-fetched. If I had a coin that was of like value to another, I could *remold* my coin in the *image* of the other. But such a ploy would only disguise its origin, not its value. If, for example, I come upon a piece of Spanish gold of similar worth, I might—by remolding it—make it appear to be an American coin."

"I can't see the advantage in that," Beede said.

"Nor can I," admitted Balfour. "After all, a Spanish coin of similar value would be accepted almost anywhere, without the need to resort to fakery."

"Nevertheless," Beede said, "there must be a reason for the existence of these strange coins. It will be interesting when we learn the truth about them."

"*If* you learn the truth," Balfour said in a dry voice, "you *must* inform me of your findings. I shall eagerly await them."

Chapter 18

"Here come Jasper," Louisa said. Glancing over his shoulder, Randolph saw the rangy, light-colored man, who seemed to be the leader of this band of refugees, striding toward them.

"Who is he?" Randolph asked.

"Jasper? He's a slave, like me. He run away from his plantation 'bout a year ago, I hear, and he's been hangin' out in the swamp since then. Whenever a slave run away, he knows to come lookin' for Jasper, and he'll help 'em hide."

Intrigued, Randolph studied the man closely as he approached. He was, perhaps, an inch or more taller than Randolph, but he weighed less, overall. His hair was curled—naturally, Randolph thought—and its color was dusky red. He could very nearly pass for white, in the proper light. Owing to the length of his feet, Jasper walked in a loopy sort of up-and-down motion, which reminded Randolph of the pitch of a boat on the ocean. He was accompanied by a motley assortment of companions.

"So, y'all had a chance to catch up on past times, now?" Jasper said on arrival. "'Cause if you is, we need to do somethin' about gettin' you somewhere safe."

"What do you have in mind?" Randolph asked.

"Well, you can always stay here, I s'pose, and join our little family, but I 'spects that don't fit your plans. Am I right 'bout that?"

"You're right," Randolph said.

"Well, then, the best thing we can do for you is to get you to a city. New Orleans all right by you?"

"That'd be fine," said Randolph. "I know my way around there, and I know people there. How're we going to get there?"

"I'll take care of that," Jasper said.

"Will we be safe there?" Louisa asked. "I ain't never been there, 'cept when I got sold, and that weren't very long. It seemed kind of big and scary."

"Honey, there ain't no place better for a nigger on the run than a big city, and there ain't no big city better for that than New Orleans," Jasper said. "There's lots of free coloreds there, so you blend in just right, 'Cept for goin' north, New Orleans is the best place to be for a slave what wants to disappear in the crowd."

"Then let's go," Randolph said. "We're ready to leave right now."

"All right, then," Jasper said. "Y'all gather up your things, whatever you're takin'. Of course," he added as they began to move away, "of course I can't go to all this trouble for nothin'."

"What you getting at?" Louisa said.

"Well, it's gon' cost some money to get you where you needs to be," Jasper said. He turned to Louisa, a sly smile crossing his face. "I figger whatever you took from ol' lady Hawkins when you done her would be just 'bout the right amount. Don't you?"

"I tole you I didn't kill her, and I didn't steal no money from her!" Louisa said, desperation in her voice. "I took a little food is all."

"Yeah, well, I knows what you said. But the old lady's dead, and the word is the money ain't there no more, so you gotta have it. I might even let you keep *some* of it, once I knows how much there is."

"There ain't no money," Louisa said. "How many times I gots to tell you?"

"If there ain't no money, I can think of one other way you can pay me," Jasper said. "In fact, you can pay me and all the boys, one at a time."

"You'll have to go through me, first," Randolph said.

"I sort of figgered that," Jasper said. "That might be fun, too. There's six of us here and only one of you. It might just whet our appetites for when Louisa serves up dessert."

Louisa moaned and sat heavily on the ground.

"Now you see what you did," Jasper said with a grin. "She's all upset. I like it when they're upset. She'll be nice and juicy now."

"There's another way," Randolph said quietly. "I have money."

"Where'd you get money?" Jasper said. "You kill somebody, too?"

"No."

"Stole it?"

"I worked for it," Randolph said. "I'm a free man, and a farmer. I've had a couple of good years, with cash crops. I've been putting money aside to buy Louisa's freedom."

"That so?" Jasper was suspicious. "How much?"

"Enough."

"I'll be the judge of that. You got it on you?"

"Here, you mean? In the swamp?"

"That's what I'm askin' you."

"Not on me, no," Randolph said. "I'm not that big a fool. But I can get it easily, once I'm back in New Orleans."

"I'm not a fool, either," Jasper said. "You go into the city and disappear, and I'll have to whistle for my money."

"Come with me, then."

"And walk into a trap? Not me. Tell you what . . . you go into New Orleans and get the money. When you come back with it, we'll let your honey lamb go."

"How do I know you won't disappear, yourself, while I'm getting the money?"

Jasper cackled. "Guess you won't. You just gots to take your chances."

"No," Randolph said. "It took me all this time to find her. I'm not letting go of her again—'specially to you."

"Well, then," Jasper said, "guess we gots ourselves a problem. How we gon' solve it?"

"Actually," Randolph said with some reluctance, "I *do* have something else you'd probably like to have. If you let Louisa go, I'll let you have it as soon as we arrive at the city."

"Oh, yeah?" Jasper said. "What's that?"

"Papers," Randolph said. "I have papers on my person that say I'm a free man."

Chapter 19

Beede had not forgotten Christmas, but he had put it out of his mind for many years. Neither Christmas nor Easter, considered, as they were, unbiblical, were observed by the Congregationalists and other reform church Protestants with whom he lived. Although he had participated in such celebrations during his years in New Orleans and Washington City (and, indeed, in Tennessee with Jackson), he had never felt completely at home with the traditions.

He felt the same ambiguous feelings of pleasure and guilt again as Dumond and his neighbors began preparations for another Christmas season of balls, theater, and dinner parties. He knew from past experience that the festivities would dominate almost every day until the holiday itself, that the season's festivities would then continue until Twelfth Night, or Epiphany, when it would meld seamlessly into Carnival, which would continue until Mardi Gras, in mid-February this year. Then would come Lent, the season of fasting and penitence, which hardly anyone in the city took seriously. After Lent would come Easter, followed by the spring social season—rather like Carnival, with balls and theater, but conducted increasingly outdoors, with the heady scent of spring flowers saturating the air. Then would come summer, when the city became hot and unbearably close, and all who could afford it would pack up their houses and move across Lake Pontchartrain until fall. Those who sought endless pleasure could do worse than to take up residence in New Orleans, where pleasure trumped most everything.

Beede, personally, was in no mood for parties and dances, but, as the guest of Pierre Dumond, his presence at such soirees was expected. And so he accompanied his host on a round of social events, which did little to lift his spirits. At every ball, young women were thrust on him by doting mothers and guardians, often (he suspected) with the knowledge—and perhaps encouragement—of Dumond himself. Beede danced the obligatory sets and invariably returned the young ladies to their mothers and aunts before excusing himself as politely as he knew how and disappearing into the throng.

All the young ladies were charming, most were well bred, some were beautiful, and a few were possessed of considerable wealth. But all were Creole and Catholic, like Adrienne, and some were, moreover, scarcely pubescent. So had been Adrienne when he had met and married her, and he had been little more than a boy himself. But he was no longer that man—that boy—and the fires of passion he had felt twenty years earlier had been banked long since. The discomfort he had always felt among women, far from disappearing as he aged, had instead grown stronger as he considered the many differences in age, and upbringing, and personalities between these fetching young ladies and himself.

It was at one of these countless balls when, after retreating to a gallery to avoid the multitudes, he came once more upon Balfour. He was leaning on the iron railing with his clay pipe, bedraggled top hat in hand, watching the crowds milling about in the street below. Beede had expected him to move away at his approach, but he did not. Instead, he nodded in more than a perfunctory way and offered up his tobacco pouch, which Beede declined as gracefully as he could.

For some time they remained side by side, in a polite if not companionable silence, watching the multitudes as they ebbed and flowed beneath them.

"Puts me in mind of Carnival," Balfour said at last. "Have you ever visited us during Carnival season?"

Beede nodded. "I lived in Louisiana for several years after reading for the law. I've seen nothing like Carnival anywhere else," he said, "although I'm told that some European cities observe similar revels."

"So they do," Balfour said. "I've been in Paris for Carnival, but not Venice. It's my understanding that Carnival in Venice is rather similar to ours in many respects."

"I've heard that, also."

"Of course, our own festivities grow more elaborate every year. I attribute it to our young men going abroad to school. They come back from France with new ideas that they cannot wait to put into practice. For example, a year or so ago they began holding parades."

"Parades?"

"Informal affairs at first, but they are becoming more sophisticated now. Someone places a notice in the *Picayune,* announcing a time and a place where the masquers should gather. Enormous crowds turn out. They march through the streets—everyone in costume—blowing horns and rattling noisemakers of all sorts. The Americans are scandalized, which makes it all quite amusing."

"I can imagine."

"There were always the balls, of course, but the parades are new. Will you be in New Orleans for Carnival, Mr. Beede?"

"I can't say," Beede replied. To himself, he said: "I hope not." He had been too long away from the farm and from New England.

"You really should remain, if your duties permit," Balfour was saying. "It is, more than ever, a pleasurable experience that should not be missed."

Balfour excused himself and departed, leaving Beede to wonder at the man's newfound civility. Was this the same man who had nearly challenged him to a duel on his first day back in the city? He appreciated the transformation, but he did not entirely trust it.

Below him, the crowds jostled and surged, like waves crashing on a shore. Beede remained a few minutes longer, watching the ebb and flow, and thinking, for reasons he could not fathom, about Deborah Tomkins and home.

Chapter 20

Christmas passed, and the city returned—as much as it ever did—to normal. Beede found himself at loose ends without Randolph, who had not yet returned from searching for Louisa. Beede had grown accustomed to his companionship, and he could not help worrying about his friend's safety—for it had been two weeks without a word.

His concern did not abate when, two days after Christmas, Conrad Schneider appeared at the door.

"I ain't heard nothing from your friend Randolph," Schneider said before Beede had had a chance to ask. "And no, I don't know what that means, or if it means anything at all. Folks who head out into the swamps without knowin' what they're doin' don't always have time to write letters of reassurance to them that worries about them."

"That's what I fear," Beede said.

"On the other hand," Schneider went on, "there usually ain't a hell of a lot out there to write home about, either. One cypress tree looks pretty much hke another."

"As do alligators," Beede said.

"This time of year, 'gators don't get around much," Schneider said. "They're the least of his worries, I expect."

Beede introduced Schneider to Pierre Dumond, who called for wine and cakes, and the three men settled into a quiet, congenial discussion. Beede was pleased to see that Dumond, unlike many Creoles, did not recoil from the thought of associating with an American, and, indeed, seemed to enjoy Schneider's company.

"I got to thinkin' about those coins I gave you," Schneider said. "You learn anything more since you got back?"

Beede recounted his conversation with Balfour, and Schneider nodded.

"So maybe they're real coins, and maybe they ain't," Schneider said. "Why am I not surprised at that?"

"The sheriff came upon two coins that appear to be American half eagles," Beede said to an obviously confused Dumond. "But they're crude-looking half eagles. Very strange in appearance."

"What's most strange," said Schneider, "is that they ain't the only ones."

"Indeed?" Beede said.

"I come up with six more, just these past two days. And I bet I'll find even more pretty soon. Matter of fact, that's why I'm here. This is where they seem to be comin' from."

"My informant at the mint assures me that the coins don't come from there," Beede said.

Schneider said, "That's what I'd say, too, if I was making coins for myself and I didn't want anyone else to know. You suppose he's tellin' the truth?"

"I hadn't thought about that," Beede said. "He *would* be in the perfect position to engage in a little counterfeiting, I suppose. How would we determine whether that is the case?"

"Good question," Schneider said. "You got me there."

Dumond, who had been silent during this exchange, finally spoke.

"Why don't you ask him?" he said.

"Don't know that he'd tell the truth about it," Schneider said.

"Nor do I," said Dumond. "But his answer might be instructive, in any event. At the very least, he would perhaps feel forced to disprove the allegation. In so doing, he might well make a mistake."

"I agree," Beede said after a moment's thought. "It's not like I can further ruin his impression of me."

"Sounds like we don't have nothin' to lose, far as I can see. We might as well give it a try," Schneider said.

This is where I leave you," Jasper said. "And I'll have those papers now."

"Not so fast," Randolph said. "Where are we, exactly?"

"You're in New Orleans," Jasper said. "Or near enough. We gots the lake to our backs. Go 'bout a mile down this path, and you'll see Bayou St. John. Keep on thataway, and you get to New Orleans."

"Can't you take us there?"

Jasper shook his head. "I cain't go there just now. One of my boys boosted a pig last week and nearly got us all caught. I gotta lay low for a little while. You'll be okay, long as you stick to the back roads."

"I'm not real comfortable with this," Randolph said.

"Don't matter to me, one way or t'other," Jasper said. "There's six of us and two of you. If you got those papers on you, we can take 'em easy enough. If it turns out you ain't got 'em, well, we'll take our pay from Louisa."

"I've got them," Randolph said, reaching for an inside coat pocket. He passed the papers to Jasper, who glanced through them and placed them inside his shirt. Randolph realized that Jasper had not studied the papers long enough to determine whether they were authentic; he suspected that Jasper could not read. *I could have given him anything,* he thought, *and Jasper would not have known the difference.* But it was no matter—even if he'd thought of it earlier, he had no other papers on his person to switch them with.

"Y'all go on now," Jasper said.

"I'll wait for you."

Jasper shrugged in indifference, and he led his party back down the path from which they had come. Randolph followed a way until he was certain that they were not doubling back before returning to Louisa.

"What'd you do that for?" she asked him, and Randolph shook his head. He had watched them for some time, and he felt it was likely that they would not follow, but he was, nevertheless, uneasy about the transac-

tion. He could acquire new papers, of course, once they
had reached New Orleans and Beede. But in the meantime, he realized, he was all too vulnerable. And Jasper
knew it.

Chapter 21

"Haven't we been through this before?" Balfour said testily. "No one is striking counterfeit coins in the United States Mint. I've told you this already."

"I know," Beede said, "but you were not quite so adamant on my previous visit."

"The question took me by surprise before," Balfour said. "I've thought about it since then, and it's my considered opinion that there cannot have been any such activity on these premises."

"I wasn't here when you talked to Mr. Beede," Schneider said. "I'd be obliged if you'd explain it all to me."

Balfour looked at him sharply. "M'sieur . . . Schneider, is it? May I inquire as to your interest in this matter?"

"He's the sheriff," Beede said. "The coins have appeared in his parish. His particular concern is that the coins seem to figure in a murder investigation."

Balfour considered this. "Nevertheless," he said, finally, "I fail to see the relevance between the appearance of coins, which may or may not be counterfeit, and a murder some distance away."

"The murdered woman was the mistress of the slave in whose possession the coins were found," said Beede. "We're trying to ascertain their origin."

"And you believe these coins have something to do with the crime?"

"We don't know!" Schneider said, his exasperation clearly on display. "That's what we're tryin' to figure out. Are *you* involved somehow? You sure are makin' this difficult if you ain't."

Balfour drew himself up to his full height. "I resent your tone, sir, as well as the implications of your question. I am employed by the national government in Washington City, and my reputation is beyond reproach."

"I have no doubt of that, sir," Beede said. "Nevertheless, these coins were minted somewhere, and this is by far the most likely place. You have the machinery, and you have the gold."

"But not the opportunity," Balfour said. "Come, I will show you what I mean."

He led the party downstairs to the building's ground floor, pointing out as he did so to the massive vaults in which bullion was stored until it was time to press it into coins.

"Every scrap of precious metal is accounted for," Balfour said. "Even the tailings from the minting procedure are returned to the refinery and melted down again. We dare not waste the least amount, of gold and silver, especially."

"Surely some is lost in the process."

"No, sir." Balfour was adamant. "Those who bring us gold for minting expect to receive the full amount back in specie. Indeed, we are forbidden by law to deduct even the expense of minting coins. This is not a profitmaking institution."

"Apparently not," said Schneider.

At ground level, Balfour showed them the stout little wooden handcarts used to transport the bullion from the vaults to the smelter. From there, they followed him upstairs to where massive rollers squeezed the metal in several passes until it was the width of a coin. The last room he led them to contained the steam-powered presses that stamped out perfect examples and sent them on for trimming, finishing, and polishing.

"I regret that I must destroy your hopes," Balfour said as their tour concluded. "But I don't believe it is possible for those crude coins of yours to have been minted in this facility."

And Beede conceded, privately, that Balfour was correct.

Strange, thought Randolph. It must be Sunday.

On a normal day, the street would be teeming with slaves going about their daily business. Today the hogs had the run of the street, with hardly a human figure in sight, and those few people who remained were anything but purposeful in their movements.

Sunday was, by long tradition, the slaves' day off.

Was it Sunday? He had lost track of time during his sojourn in the swamps, but he was fairly certain it was not.

Louisa noticed it, too. "This supposed to be a big city," she said with a trace of asperity in her voice. "Where's all the people?"

"I don't know," he said. "There ought to be many people about by this time of morning. I'll have to ask someone."

"Is that wise?"

"I'll be careful who I ask."

The buildings in this part of town were ramshackle wood-frame affairs, unlike the brick-between-posts structures in the old section of the city, with their stucco coverings designed to protect the soft native brick from wind and weather. He studied the signs as they walked: stores selling leeches, dry goods, paint and hardware, up ahead a livery stable, a barber, the signs written in a variety of English and French, sometimes both, producing a scrambled, ungrammatical bouillabaisse that approximated an entirely different idiom.

Where *were* the people to whom these signs are directed? he asked himself again.

It might be too early for the Creole gentlemen and their ladies, but surely the slaves should be up and about. He began searching his memory for occasions on which slaves might have been relieved of their responsibilities. There were not so very many: Christmas and New Year's Day were both long past. Easter—not yet come, and on a Sunday, besides. Washington's birthday—the right time of year, but not normally cause for a major work stoppage. What else?

Mardi Gras.

The realization brought him to a sudden halt, causing Louisa, who was walking a few steps behind, to stumble into him. Of course, Mardi Gras was widely considered reason enough to malinger. Various attempts had been made to outlaw Mardi Gras celebrations, particularly since the Americans had arrived in such numbers, but the habit was long ingrained in the local consciousness, and the attempts had failed. The city, it was said, had even been founded on Mardi Gras.

Randolph thought. Could Mardi Gras be used to their advantage? Perhaps, if they were in costume, they would be less identifiable to anyone who was seeking them—and he had no doubt that someone *would* be seeking them. That was why Jasper accepted his papers with such equanimity. Somewhere—probably somewhere nearby—lay a slave-taker with whom Jasper had an agreement. No doubt he received a commission on each slave—putative slave—he delivered, as well as an assurance of safety for himself and his band of refugees.

People of color were not permitted to mask, for fear that slaves might use the anonymity of the occasion as an opportunity to flee from bondage. Randolph wasn't sure what this would mean to his prospects for his and Louisa's safe passage, but he knew that the situation warranted an extra measure of caution.

They continued down along the Esplanade Ridge, where the Creole world reigned supreme and the detestable "Kaintucks," as the Creoles called virtually all Americans of Anglo descent, were rarely if ever encountered. Randolph liked it that way. He suspected Creoles were less inclined to view all people of color as potential slaves and would therefore be less concerned about people of color walking together unaccompanied.

As they neared the river they began to encounter crowds of people. Young, boisterous Creole gentlemen crowded the wooden sidewalks, walking three and four abreast, arm in arm, taking great delight in forcing others to step into the muddy, dung-spattered street. Many—perhaps most—of the young men were already deep in their cups, although the sun was not yet much above the rooftops

Mardi Gras, thought Randolph. It is definitely Mardi Gras, or very near to it. Near enough to that holiday that useful work has come to a halt. I must think on how I can make use of this.

Nothing had occurred to him by the time they had reached Dumond's wineshop and house on Rue Royale. Avoiding the street entrance, they passed down the alley to a door that led to the courtyard. There he knocked on the door for what seemed to him like hours before the young servant girl finally appeared and, with a brief curtsy, showed them into the house. Randolph found himself wondering briefly if Dumond had no other servants.

The girl disappeared as silently as she had come, leaving them standing just inside the door.

"Where is we?" Louisa asked, looking around her with undisguised curiosity.

"Somewhere safe," Randolph replied. "I hope."

Beede was first to appear, followed closely—Randolph was surprised to see him—by Schneider and, a few minutes later, by Dumond. It took some time to explain to Louisa who these people were and to allay her fears.

"By rights, I suppose, I *should* be arresting you for murder," Schneider said, answering her unspoken question. "Problem is, I don't think you killed her. Takin' you back with me would take the pressure off me to find the real killer, but I wouldn't feel right about it."

"I ain't killed nobody!" Louisa said.

"Like I said," Schneider repeated patiently, "I don't think you did. But maybe you remember somethin' that would help me find the right person."

"Like what?"

Schneider shook his head. "I don't know," he admitted. "I'm just feelin' my way in the dark with this. You worked with ol' Miz Hawkins. Who mighta wanted her dead?"

"I can't think of nobody, sir. She didn't hardly ever have visitors, and she didn't have nothing much that anybody'd want, either. 'Ceptin' slaves, I s'pose."

"What about land?"

"I guess land, too, but I expect it's pretty much played out. It's cotton land, you knows, and cotton land wears out purty fast."

Schneider scratched the back of his head.

"You see, the thing is," he said slowly, "you bein' a slave, you got a natural reason for killin' your mistress. I don't think you did it, but I can't come up with anybody else who might be a suspect. And you ain't helpin' much."

"That's 'cause I don't know nothin'."

"There's the overseer," Beede pointed out. "What's his name, Travis?"

"True," said Schneider. "We ain't found him, and I don't think we will. But you're right, he might be a suspect." To Louisa he said, "Did you kill ol' Travis? Maybe he try to do you so you did him first?"

"Travis?" Louisa said, her voice rising to a wail. "Now you thinks I killed Travis, too? I ain't never killed *nobody*. That's God's honest truth."

"But you got the motive," Schneider reminded her. "So right now, you're all I got."

Dumond put them up in his house, although he did so with obvious reluctance. Louisa retired early; the stress of the past few days clearly had taken their toll, and she went off to sleep in the kitchen alongside Dumond's own cook. After some consideration, Dumond permitted Randolph to bed down on the floor at the foot of Beede's bed in the room he had occupied with Adrienne after their marriage.

"I can't let them take Louisa away from me again," Randolph said frantically that night, when they were alone. "I can't believe that she's a murderer, but I don't think she'll get the benefit of the doubt."

"I think Sheriff Schneider is an honest man," Beede said. "If it's up to him, no innocent person will be bullied into a false conviction."

"I don't think it will be up to him," Randolph said. "And I must tell you further that I don't care whether she is innocent or guilty. I'm prepared to spirit her away from this place, regardless. I would appreciate your assistance, but I will do without it if I must."

"You put me in a delicate position," Beede said. "I've given my life to the law, as you know. But it's early, yet. Let us wait a while. Perhaps we can find another way."

"I hope that you are right," Randolph said after a moment. "But I doubt very much that you are." And he rolled over on his pallet to face the wall.

Chapter 22

Beede lay awake much of the night considering what Randolph had said, and by morning he found himself in agreement. It made considerable sense to leave the city now. If they stayed together, they might be able to pull it off. They had come for Louisa, and now they had her. It was true that she was still a slave, but it was not clear that she actually belonged to anyone. Her owner was dead and apparently had no heirs. It was conceivable that some provision had been made for the disposition of her slaves in Esther Hawkins's will—if she had made one—but it might be months before the disposition of her estate would be settled. Meanwhile, the time for planting was rapidly approaching. It was urgent that they return to New England.

And if a dispute were to arise at some later date? Well, he reminded himself, possession was nine tenths of the law. Any lawsuit would be played out in New England, where the right judge might be amenable to argument. There were not many antislavery judges in New England, despite the fact that slavery was illegal there, but there were a few. By the time such a case was brought to court, there might well be more.

He brought the matter up with Dumond in the morning and was surprised to find him in agreement as well.

"It serves no purpose for you to remain here," Dumond said. "Matters such as these can be drawn out for a long time, and there is no certainty to the result. If you were attempting to escape justice, it might be a different matter, but to this date no one has come searching for the girl. The sooner you leave, the safer you are likely to be."

Schneider was less acquiescent, for Louisa was, in name at least, still a murder suspect.

"I don't think she's guilty," he said. "I told you that before. But I can't rule her out completely. I'm not too thrilled to have her take off to New England, out of my reach, if I need her."

"If a jury found her guilty, what would happen to her?" Beede said. "Would she be hanged?"

"Not likely. She's not free colored; she's property. Most likely she'd be sold."

"That's what I thought," Beede said. "We'll buy her. It's what we intended at the outset."

"And if someone comes seeking her?"

"Say she's been sold. A buyer appeared, and you sold her."

Reluctantly, Schneider agreed to accept three hundred dollars for Louisa. With her status thus seemingly assured, the little party made haste to get on their way.

Beede and Randolph had brought little baggage with them, and Louisa had nothing but the clothes on her back, so it did not take long. Schneider followed along at a distance to watch for trouble.

They emerged into a street pulsating with life. Though it was still early, crowds swarmed the streets, bringing horse traffic to a standstill. Celebrants were forming themselves into the informal parades that Balfour had told him about. Beede's little party was becoming uncomfortably conspicuous, and he could sense Louisa's growing apprehensiveness at the noise and the commotion.

"Quickly, come with me!" Pierre Dumond said.

"Where are we going?" Beede asked.

"We're joining the parade."

He fled down an alley to a courtyard entrance, Beede, Randolph, and Louisa hurrying behind. At the courtyard he opened a door and motioned them inside.

"Find a costume," he said. "Don't worry about a perfect fit! Hurry!"

"Where are we?" Beede asked.

"Backstage," Dumond said. The room was filled with old wardrobe trunks, all of them standing open, contents scattered about like the aftermath of a looting. Beede saw a harlequin, a suit of armor, a medieval princess, a polar bear. He passed the princess costume to Louisa, while Randolph held up a Chanticleer for inspection.

"I could almost fit in this," he said. "But my face will show. They'll know I'm not a white man."

"Do not worry," Dumond said. "It is Mardi Gras. No one will know."

"How can they *not* know?"

"It will be taken care of. Hurry and dress. When you have finished, put your clothing in this. You will need them again later," he said, handing them a burlap bag smelling of green coffee beans.

When they had changed into their costumes—Beede had chosen the brown robe of a Capuchin friar—Dumond, who had chosen to go as Cardinal Richelieu, had them stand together in a group while he threw handfuls of flour in their faces.

"Always at Carnival, young rakes prowl the streets with bags of flour, throwing it into the faces of masquers. We are merely saving them the trouble. Now, someone throw some of this flour at me; it would not do for one of us to be conspicuously different from the others."

Dumond went ahead of the others to ensure that it was safe to leave the building. Upon reflection, Beede concluded later that it wouldn't have mattered, for the street was jammed with men, women, and children, in and out of costume, jumping and dancing and blowing discordant notes on trumpets and clarinets. Here and there Beede could make out the strains of a popular tune, but no two celebrants, it appeared, were playing the same tune, in the same key, and some were blowing merely to produce noise.

They joined the march down Rue Royale. Dumond fell in step beside Beede.

"When we reach Esplanade, we will turn to the right and proceed toward the river," Dumond said. "We can hire passage on a boat there."

"You're coming with us?"

"A short distance only. I must return to my shop.

Lent begins tomorrow, after all, and business will return
to normal."

"Thank you for all you have done for us, Pierre. We
will be forever in your debt. I know Randolph shares
my gratitude."

"No thanks are necessary. I have always liked Randolph. He, more than anyone I know, deserves to be a
free man, with a wife and family."

"Nevertheless, it is most unexpected of you," Beede
said. "And gratifying."

"Yes, it is unexpected, isn't it? Please don't expect it
in the future. I'm doing this for you and for Randolph,
not because I oppose slavery."

They proceeded as cautiously as possible without
drawing attention to themselves. At Esplanade, they
turned, as Dumond had suggested, and moved as a
group toward the levee. The crowds were less dense
here, and Beede had the sense that their little band was
far more conspicuous than it had been only moments
earlier.

But the levee was not far now, and steamboats were
waiting there, huffing and panting like impatient horses
as the passengers milled around at the gangplanks. Dumond went ahead of the party and purchased passage
for three to Cincinnati. They said their farewells then,
and the small party began to board.

They did not get far. As they stepped on the gang-
plank a shout arose, and Beede turned to see a round little white man waddling toward them, accompanied by
two tall men in long frock coats and armed with muskets.

"You and Louisa should go quickly," Beede said

with a sense of foreboding. "Get on board, and I'll deal with these men."

Randolph shook his head sadly. "They won't let us board if you aren't accompanying us," he said. "Not even with a ticket."

It no longer mattered, for the posse—Beede was certain it was a posse—had arrived.

"Well, we have arrived just in time, I see," the round man said with a smile. "I feared that you might have made a clean break of it."

"This young wench must be my poor late aunt's murderer, he said, looking closely at Louisa. "No, girl, you've never met me, but I certainly have heard of you. My old Aunt Esther was so pleased to acquire you, and how did you repay her kindness? By killing her and stealing her property? Shame." He shook his head in mock sorrow.

And he turned to Randolph. For a moment, Beede thought he detected confusion in the man's eyes. If so, he recovered quickly.

"And Toby!" he said delightedly. "What a pleasant surprise! I had given up hope of ever seeing you again after you vanished from the plantation. I should have known that you would seek out the lovely Louisa before you made good your escape. Or did *she* seek *you?*"

He gestured to the two guards who accompanied him. "Officers, please take these two slaves into custody. I will appear shortly to redeem them and return them to the plantation."

"I must protest!" Beede shouted. "These people are not slaves!"

The guards hurried Randolph and Louisa away at gunpoint, and the round man turned to Beede.

"Your name is Beede, is it not?" he said.

"Yes."

He nodded with a smile of satisfaction.

"I will deal with you later," he said. "You can be assured of that."

Chapter 23

"It just goes to show," Schneider was saying, leaning back in his chair in the center courtyard of Pierre Dumond's house on Rue Royale, "you can never predict the future worth a lick. I was fairly sure I'd be on my way back home by this time, but here I am still."

"This isn't your battle," Beede said as Dumond poured the coffee. "There's no reason for you to hang around while we sort this matter out. I, for one, am pleased to have you here, but I realize you have your duties to see to."

"Actually," Schneider said with a frown, "I suspect this *is* my duty, somehow. I don't pretend to understand what's goin' on, but I think it's all got somethin' to do with the murder of ol' lady Hawkins, and *that* is certainly my problem. This Devall fella claims to be her nephew, you say?"

"That is his claim."

"It should not be so very difficult to determine the truth of that assertion," Dumond said. "If there is a will, there would be documents."

"Should be," Schneider said. "Our parish records are in such a muddle, though, that they might be lost. I'll send word back home and have someone check on that for you."

"He *may* have a claim on Louisa," Beede said. "Someone almost certainly does. He can't have any sort of claim on Randolph, however. I freed Randolph myself, three years ago."

"Can you prove it, though?" Schneider said mildly.

"Randolph and I both carried copies of his freedom papers, specifically to ward off this sort of thing," Beede said. "Both sets are now missing. Randolph says his papers were taken from him during his journey out of the swamp. My copy was taken when I went to the Cabildo to see to his release. They were not returned, and Randolph was not freed, even into my custody."

"Without papers it will certainly prove difficult to prevail in court," Dumond said. "Are there no corroborating witnesses upon whom you can call?"

"None that come to mind. At least, not in New Orleans."

"Maybe that was the plan all along," Schneider said, sipping his coffee with a frown. "Louisa's a pretty little thing, but Randolph'd be worth a lot more money on the market. A big, strong darkie like him with no defects—you could name your own price for a boy like that."

"He's not for sale," Beede said. "I wouldn't sell him even if I could."

"Oh, I know that," Schneider said. "But many a man—a *southern* white man—wouldn't think twice about pullin' off a fiddle like this. When they see a slave they don't see a man; they see livestock on the hoof. I'm just sayin' that maybe Randolph's the one this Devall gent is most interested in."

"I doubt that," Beede said. "Who would know about Randolph? Someone may have seen him around the town, but how would anyone know who he was or that he no longer possessed papers of manumission? It seems unlikely, in the extreme."

"This Jasper fella, that he told us about, might be the missing link in the chain," Schneider pointed out. "Devall might know Randolph doesn't have his papers because Jasper told him so."

Beede considered Schneider's words for a moment before speaking. "So if what you say is true, then this Toby person that Devall referred to is made up? That this is all a ruse?"

"Yep, that'd be my guess," Schneider said. "Devall's tryin' to muddy the waters a bit, shift the burden from him to you. This way he doesn't have to prove that Randolph isn't a free man; *you* have to prove that he isn't a slave named Toby."

"How can I do that, if Toby doesn't exist?"

"Only way that I can see," Schneider said, "is to prove that he *is* Randolph. Damned if I know how you can do that."

Later that evening, Pierre Dumond sat alone by the dwindling embers of the fire in his parlor, pondering his friend's difficulties. He had no strong feelings for or against slavery, although he had grown up with slaves ever present to do his bidding. Without a wife, or children, he found that he could get along very well with minimal assistance and he had, as a consequence, reduced his household staff accordingly.

Briefly he considered his own situation. Could he, like Beede, free his two remaining servants and continue to live in something approximating his present circumstances? He had no intention of doing so, but he wondered if it would even be possible.

Finding that prospect too horrifying to think about, he quickly turned to the question that followed naturally: If he were to free his slaves, who would have to know about it?

At the very least, he thought, there would be records somewhere. Manumission was not unheard of, but it was sufficiently infrequent that independent corroboration would be required.

And where would that corroboration be found? Beede and Randolph lived now in New England. That would be the place to begin the search.

He could hardly go to New England himself; he had a business to run. But there was a girl, he remembered. She had written to Beede, who had made little of their correspondence but who was obviously flattered . . . and clearly interested.

Would she be willing to help from afar? Was she clever enough to know where to look, or even to understand the situation sufficiently? It was Dumond's impression, based on his conversations with Beede, that New England girls were sent to school alongside their brothers and were mostly literate. The letter, what he

had seen of it over Beede's shoulder, implied a high
level of literacy.

It was worth a try. Dumond sat at his desk with pen
and inkwell and began writing. He remembered the address, which, in any event, was not difficult. Deborah . . . Tomkins! Yes, that was the name. At Tomkins
Farm, Warrensboro, New Hampshire.

> *Dear Miss Tomkins,*
>   *I am writing to you as a long time friend of a mu-*
> *tual acquaintance, Josiah Beede. I believe he re-*
> *quires assistance that you may be able to*
> *provide. . . .*

He labored many hours on the text of the letter,
struggling for precision in a language that was less familiar to him than his native French, even after nearly
thirty years of American occupation. When he was
done, he sealed the letter and climbed the stairs to bed,
feeling that he had performed a useful task.

Lent began the following morning. The time of fasting and atonement was marked chiefly by an un-
customary period of quiet. In the early afternoon, after
the residents of the city had returned from worship,
Beede, accompanied by Schneider, trudged to the Cabildo in the hope of visiting Randolph and Louisa. They
were turned back by a guard who was clearly suffering
from the repercussions of an extended celebration on
the previous day.

Remonstration proved futile even after Beede took

his case to higher authorities. In the aftermath of Carnival, hardly anyone was prepared to plunge headlong into the dreary routine of business. Beede found the experience frustrating and said as much to Schneider.

"Come back tomorrow. Come back tomorrow," Beede said heatedly. "It is all they will tell me. What shall I do? What *can* I do?"

Schneider gave the question a moment's thought.

"Offhand," he said, "you should probably come back tomorrow."

Several tomorrows passed before Beede was finally admitted to see his friend. Randolph looked surprisingly well, Beede thought, considering his ordeal.

No, he said, he had not been beaten yet. Since his status was unclear, the city authorities were perhaps reluctant to damage what could conceivably be a valuable property. Ironically, if they were certain he was a free man, he would have been beaten severely long before now, Beede thought.

"I'm worried about Louisa," Randolph said. "She has lived a sheltered life, for a slave. She grew up in Alexandria and has had but one owner prior to this Mrs. Hawkins. She must be frightened half to death; I know *I* am."

"I intend to visit her next," Beede said. "Do you have any message that you would wish me to pass along to her?"

"Only that I love her. Tell her that, please."

"I'm certain that will bring her some comfort," Beede said, wondering that he had not heard Randolph say those words before. He wondered if Louisa had.

In any event, the words did not console Louisa as Beede had expected. She received him civilly enough in her cell, but on hearing Randolph's message she turned from Beede and erupted in a spasm of tears and wails. Beede could get no more from her, and he was forced to leave her in a state of anguish for which he could find no explanation.

The court hearing concerning Louisa's status began on Friday, and it began as badly as Beede had feared. Devall was, of course, present with his attorney, a bluff, red-haired, pink-faced man who identified himself as James Harrison and who was obviously well known to the court.

Harrison began aggressively, challenging not merely Beede's assertions but also Randolph's status as a witness and Beede's proposal to serve as his counsel.

"Your Honor, I must protest," Harrison said. "Are we to take the word of a colored man, a former slave, over that of a distinguished Creole gentleman? Surely Mr. Devall's testimony must merit more consideration than the unsupported statements of this colored boy. How do we even know that he *is* a free man?"

"Mr. Beede, do you care to respond on your client's behalf?"

"Mr. Randolph is, indeed, a free man, Your Honor. I have personal knowledge of that, for I am the man who freed him."

"Would you be willing to attest to this under oath?"

"Of course."

"Your Honor, this is all very well," said Harrison, "but it is still the unsupported allegation of a man who is a stranger to us all. And even if the court is prepared to accept this allegation at its face, it cannot extend its credence to encompass the woman as well. Mr. Devall is prepared to call additional witnesses to support his contention that the woman is, and has been, his family's personal property for several years."

"Mr. Beede?"

"Your Honor, Randolph and I have lived in the North for many years and have few acquaintances remaining here. M'sieur Pierre Dumond, wine merchant of Rue Royale, knows us both, however, and can offer witness to our characters."

"Can he support your assertion that the boy here is a free man?"

"Indirectly, yes. We have discussed Mr. Randolph's status many times."

"And the young woman?"

"Hearsay!" Harrison shouted. "Clearly, M'sieur Dumond knows only what Mr. Beede has told him. Hardly unimpeachable evidence."

"If Your Honor is prepared to wait," Beede began, "I can seek affidavits from people who know Mr. Randolph well. These men are New Englanders, so it would be necessary to contact them by post, and their replies would of necessity require several weeks' time—"

"Your Honor"—Harrison was almost whining now—"surely this court must not rely on the unsupported testimony of Yankees! The northern attitude toward slavery is well known. Do we not receive their abolitionist tracts every month, despite the laws prohibiting such dissemination in the slave states? Such men would assert that the devil himself is a free man if by so doing they could strike a blow against slavery!"

"By all accounts, Satan *is* a free man," Beede said. "I

know of no passage in Scripture that asserts that he is anything else."

"Your Honor!"

"Save your indignation for the stump, Jamie," the judge said. "I'm a good Catholic, and I've no need for one of your hell-raising sermons." He turned back to Beede. "Mr. Harrison has been attending too many Protestant tent revivals," he said. "An occupational hazard, no doubt, for a man who trades with Americans. Nevertheless he has a point. Can you offer any valid evidence—*southern* evidence—to justify your contention?"

"Your Honor, I personally manumitted Mr. Randolph in gratitude for many years of faithful service. He was a gift from my wife's family on the occasion of our wedding. It was within my power—and in no one else's—to grant his freedom. My word should be sufficient proof, under the circumstances."

"And I say that this boy's name is not Randolph, but Toby, and he has belonged to my client's family for nigh on to twenty years now," Harrison said. "Let Mr. Beede disprove that, if he can."

"Mr. Randolph came to New Orleans in full possession of his freedom papers," Beede replied. "Unfortunately, they were taken from him when we were detained on Mardi Gras."

"Is that true, Jamie?"

"Your Honor, Mr. Beede and this nigger boy were stopped in the act of smuggling another slave out of the city—a slave who was wanted for questioning concerning the murder of her mistress. Although papers were found in Mr. Beede's possession, it was reasonable to assume that this boy's papers were forged."

"Where are these papers now?"

"We burned them so they would not cause further mischief."

The judge turned to Beede. "Have you no other copies of these papers, sir? It would be truly reckless to bring only one set with you."

"Randolph and I each had a set in our possession in anticipation of this very confusion," Beede said. "Those papers were taken from me."

"How awkward and inconvenient," Harrison said dryly. "Considering the importance of these alleged papers, one would have thought they would not have been treated in so cavalier a fashion. A certain amount of care should have been taken to see to it that they were not misplaced."

"They were not misplaced, Your Honor," Beede said. "They were taken from me."

Harrison snorted. The judge frowned at him from the bench.

"And where are these papers now?" the judge asked.

"I do not know, Your Honor. I know only that they were not returned, and those who took them denied all knowledge of them, even though the transaction had taken place less than an hour earlier."

"Mr. Beede, your story is far too fantastical to be countenanced. Would you have us believe that you and your colored friend here are the victims of some sort of conspiracy?"

"It is difficult for me to believe, as well, Your Honor, but the conclusion is inescapable."

Harrison almost squealed in protest.

"Your Honor, must we hear more of this farfetched

tale? I request a ruling from the bench to bring these proceedings to a halt."

"You shall not have it, Jamie. Not yet, at least."

"Mr. Harrison is quite correct in at least one respect, sir," the judge said, addressing his remarks to Beede. "And I would be inclined to honor his request, except for one small matter: I tend to distrust such a piling-on of coincidence after coincidence."

"Perhaps it isn't coincidence at all."

"Would you care to explain that remark, sir? It sounds suspiciously like contempt of court."

"I do not mean it in that way, Your Honor. I do not doubt the court's integrity, but I question whether these events were not planned by someone with underhanded motives. If the court will permit, I would appreciate an opportunity to investigate the matter further."

The judge frowned. "I do not intend to prolong these proceedings any longer than is absolutely necessary. But neither do I wish to deprive a free man of that freedom, if it can be proved. How much time do you require?"

"I believe two months would be a reasonable time," Beede said. "It will take some time for correspondence to make its way to New England and back, and my acquaintances also will need some time to collect the evidence."

"Your Honor!"

"Silence, Jamie. Your objections are noted. Mr. Beede, I will give you six weeks, no more. I cannot continue this matter forever."

It was less time than he had hoped for but more than he had expected. "Thank you, Your Honor," he said.

"This court is in recess. We shall hold the boy Randolph as surety in the interim."

The judge banged his gavel. Beede turned to go, but the judge called to him from the bench.

"It would be wise, sir, not to depend entirely on your friends in New England," the judge said. "If you cannot find southern evidence to support your case, I fear your situation is dire. The evidence of Yankees is rightly considered suspect in these parts."

Chapter 24

Another Sunday came, blessed, like most days at this time of year, with sunshine, early magnolia blossoms, and the promise of a spectacular spring to come. Beede took the opportunity to stroll down to the river, sit on an empty handcart, and stare at the current.

He had arisen earlier than anyone else in the household in order to be alone to think. In New Hampshire, the relative peace that surrounded him every day left ample opportunities to be alone with his thoughts. Here, in this bustling, polyglot seaport city, solitude was a luxury he often sought, but rarely found.

And today he needed solitude to think about the problems that beset him, which seemed amenable to no solution he could imagine. When he and Randolph had set out from Warrensboro the previous fall, Beede had not conceived of the difficulties they would encounter.

And while he had suspected even then that the tasks they had set for themselves would not be easily accomplished, matters had gone disastrously awry in ways he had not anticipated.

First, they had arrived in Alexandria, Virginia, where Randolph and Louisa had met and married, only to discover that she had been sold down the river. Making their way to New Orleans, where most slaves were destined, they found that Louisa had been bought for service on a downriver plantation. Having journeyed to that plantation, they discovered that Louisa was missing and her new mistress slain. Now both she and Randolph had been captured and held as runaways.

It seemed there was little he could do to rectify the situation. He would continue to represent the couple in court to the best of his ability, but people of color had few legal rights, even when free. If their freedom were in dispute, even those meager rights might be wiped away as if they had never existed.

A sudden gust of wind, surprisingly cold considering that it was almost the end of March, wrenched his thoughts back to the present. He had come to the river to think, but this mode of thought was accomplishing little of value. It led him in circles and deposited him in a morass of despair. What was needed here, he concluded, was some systematic contemplation of the circumstances.

When forced to unravel a knotty problem, he had long since learned to extract those elements that seemed to be extraneous in order to arrive at the nub. But what was extraneous, and what *was* the nub?

The nub, he concluded, was that he lacked sufficient information. Forces of which he was unaware were working toward ends he did not understand. Who were they, and where were they acquiring their information?

The day's first dockworkers—an interracial assortment indeed—were beginning to trickle in from wherever they had chosen to spend the night. Many, clearly, had spent their nights in the city's brothels and taverns, in the bed of a whore or under a taproom table. Beede was forced to move from his handcart, which was needed. He walked to the riverbank, dodging work crews as he went, and watched the activity from an out-of-the way location.

"Enjoying the sunshine, sir?"

The voice startled him from his thoughts, and he looked up to see an immaculately dressed man standing before him, smiling broadly. It took Beede a moment before he recognized him as the man who had intervened on the quay when they had arrived in New Orleans.

"Yes, I am," Beede said, returning the smile, standing and offering his hand. "I'm happy to encounter you again, particularly since I hadn't an opportunity to introduce myself before. I'm Josiah Beede, from New Hampshire."

"Nathaniel Prescott," the man said. "Tennessee. I'm pleased to make the acquaintance of the famous boy hero of New Orleans. Your fame precedes you, as you see."

"Ah," Beede said, embarrassed, "I fear you are laboring under a delusion. My actions at Chalmette were hardly heroic. If I had been thinking clearly, rather than being frightened and angry, I should never have picked up a gun at all."

"It's been my experience," Prescott said, "that few

men would be heroic if they had a minute to think about it. Nevertheless, I've no desire to discomfit you, and I shall say no more about it, if that's your wish. Tell me why you're back in this libertine, Catholic city. You were a New England Yankee then, if I remember aright."

"I was, and I am. I'm here for a brief time only, on some personal business. And you, sir?"

"I'm a cotton factor, and I represent a number of plantations along the river. My home is in Memphis, upriver, but my business regularly takes me to New Orleans."

"The plantations are upstream and downstream, but not here in the city," Beede said.

"But the banks are here," Prescott said. "I daresay New Orleans has more banks per person than any other city in the country. A planter's representative might go for many days without handling cotton, but it's much more difficult to avoid handling money."

"I suppose that's so."

"Of course," Prescott went on, "more and more planters are turning to sugar rather than cotton, especially downstream. The profit margin is greater, although there's also more risk, and you go through slaves much faster. The work quickly wears men down."

"I've heard that sugar growing is much riskier than cotton," Beede said. "You must build sugar mills, which are expensive, and you need much more growing land than for cotton."

"Cotton is risky business as well," Prescott said. "But you're right; to make your fortune producing sugar, you would be well advised to buy out all your neighbors on all sides. You'll need that extra acreage to grow enough to break even. There's an old saying: 'It takes a rich cotton planter to make a poor sugar planter.'"

A question occurred to Beede: if Prescott were a cotton factor, and dependent on the good will of planters, why had he defended Randolph during the incident on the levee?

"Do you remember the man with whom I argued on my first day here, on the levee?" he asked Prescott. "I realize it has been some months since we met, but—"

"Achille Balfour, from the mint. I remember. He's well known in New Orleans. What is your concern with him? Does he bother you still?"

"On the contrary, he has been most helpful in . . . a certain matter. In fact, it is that helpfulness that concerns me, given that he was anything but pleasant at our first meeting. It's almost as if he were a different person; he doesn't go out of his way to be convivial, but he is never less than civil."

"Probably it was your colored companion who set him off that first day," Prescott said. "For as long as I've known him—and I've known him for many years— Achille has always borne an inordinate distaste for the colored race. He doesn't own slaves himself, far as I can determine, and he seems to hold a grudge for those who do, and for the slaves, themselves, and for free people of color also. It's quite indiscriminate, this revulsion."

"Do you have any idea of the cause?"

Prescott spread his hands as if to express a bemused puzzlement. "No idea, I fear," he said. "I've had the sense, once or twice, that he fears people of color and wants to keep his distance from them."

"Is it rebellion he fears? Is he afraid that Nat Turner will rise up and slay him in his bed?"

"Well, they hanged ol' Nat seven years ago, so I doubt that Achille is worried about him anymore, although if it's insurrection he's concerned about, there's plenty more where that one came from. No, in Achille's case it's more like he's afraid that they know some secret that can destroy him. I don't know what it might be; can't pin it down any closer than that."

"What could a black man—free or not—do to a free white man?"

"A very good question, indeed," Prescott replied. "I'm as perplexed as you."

"Thank you for your assistance on that day."

"Happy to have obliged you," Prescott said. "Pleased to make your acquaintance, as well. If there's anything I can do for you, don't hesitate to come to me. You can find me right here, most days, at least until I head back upstream to Memphis."

Prescott tipped his brim and ambled slowly across the quay. Beede watched him depart for a few minutes before he turned and began his return to Dumond's house.

Chapter 25

It was difficult to find a comfortable place to sleep in the cells. She had thought, after her experience in the swamp, that she would be able to sleep in any situation. Apparently she was wrong. The pallet of straw on the cold brick floor swarmed with vermin and did little to cushion the hard surface. She was tired and wanted desperately to sleep—perhaps forever.

"Louisa? That you?"

A woman's voice, from a nearby cell. A familiar voice, though she could not think why.

"Louisa, honey, it's Lucy. From the swamp. Remember?"

In her mind Louisa saw once again the slim, angular woman who had taken her part during the debate at Jasper's runaway camp. She had shown herself to be a friend in that situation.

"Lucy? Where you at? What you doin' here?"

"I'se about two doors down from you, I think. I got picked up on the road one night—musta been last Thursday, now. I'se losin' track of the days in here."

"I'se sorry to hear that," Louisa said. "I was just thinkin' about Jasper and the camp and how safe I felt when I was there."

"Well, don't get yourself too worked up about that," Lucy said. "Jasper done sold me down the river. He'd a' done the same to you if he'd had the chance."

"Sold you down the river? How'd he do that?"

"He's the one sent me out that night," Lucy said. "He tol' me Tansy had squirreled away some fatback that the mistress would never miss. He said Tansy was savin' it for us and I should go pick it up."

"Sounds like somethin' Tansy would do."

"It do, don't it? Only when I got there Tansy said she'd never heard of it, and she didn't have nothin' for us. That made me suspicious, and sure enough, on the way back to camp the pattyrollers was waitin'."

"So he set you up."

"Like a pigeon. Leastwise, that's the way it looks, and I can't ask him about it 'cause I'se in this jail and he's outside."

"But why? Nobody's gon' believe him if he does that. He gets known for double dealin', who's gon' come to him for help?"

"I don't know," Lucy said. "Onliest thing I can think of is . . . maybe he don't care no more. Maybe he's got somethin' big in the works and he don't need us now."

"What could that be?" Louisa said.

"Don't know that, nuther," Lucy replied. "But it'd have to be somethin' real big."

• • •

The next six weeks passed more quickly than he had hoped. Beede passed the time by writing to long-time acquaintances in a fruitless quest for corroboration. In desperation he sought out local lawyers who might be prepared to assist him. But while some expressed sympathies with Randolph's plight, none were able to suggest strategies.

Court resumed. Beede was no better prepared to defend Randolph—much less Louisa—than when it had recessed six weeks earlier. He had written to people he knew in New Hampshire—people who could confirm that Randolph was a free man—but had not heard from anyone. And even if he had heard from them, he admitted to himself, New Hampshire people were Yankees and, as such, were not likely to be deemed credible by a Louisiana court.

Nor had he heard from Schneider, who had promised to look for Esther Hawkins's will in the parish records, to determine whether the man who claimed to be her nephew was mentioned at all. But Schneider had admitted that parish records were in disarray, and he had hinted that they might not be forthcoming. In frustration Beede had returned to the parish himself to assist in the search—another futile task.

So he went to court and begged for a continuance.

"Mr. Beede, you were warned that I cannot continue this case indefinitely," the judge said. "You have had six weeks already."

"I'm aware of that, Your Honor. I'm expecting new information momentarily, but the mails have not yet delivered it. I'm certain it will be here by the end of the week." It was, if not a lie, the next thing to it. He was desperate, and he knew it.

He had the sense that the judge knew it, too, but he granted another week.

"I'm granting your request specifically because you've represented to me that the necessary proofs are on their way," the judge admonished him. "If they are not here when we reconvene next Monday, I'm inclined to hold you to account."

"I understand, Your Honor. And thank you."

As he left the courtroom, his eye caught Harrison's. The opposing attorney smiled and tipped his hat.

"Until Monday," he said with a feline grin, and Beede felt his cheeks burning until he reached the street.

Dumond was waiting for him outside, and he saw, from Beede's countenance, that events had not gone well.

"At least I've bought another week," Beede said, "although for the life of me I can't imagine what I can do with it."

"It may, perhaps, be time to consider flight," Dumond said. "I hesitate to suggest it, but it's clear to me that you are in the right of this, and it's equally clear that the odds are not in your favor. It's a sad irony that breaking the law may be the only way to ensure justice."

"Surely Devall and his cronies will be watching the roads and the port," Beede said. "Moreover, Randolph and Louisa are still in chains. I suspect that it's too late to make our escape. We should have done so weeks ago, but I had faith that we would find a way to resolve the dilemma."

"Then what will you do?"

"I don't know," Beede said. "I cannot afford to give up hope, and yet I see no solution at hand."

They parted company at the corner, Beede to visit Randolph in the cells, which were in the rear of the building, and Dumond to the river to inspect a newly arrived shipment of wine.

Beede found Randolph in a depressed mood—unsurprising under the circumstances—pacing the floor of his cell, head down, hands clasped behind his back.

"I have tried not to become discouraged," Randolph said, "but it has become increasingly difficult to maintain my optimism. I hope you have good news for me."

"Would that I had," Beede said. "I am searching in every place I can think of, but New Hampshire is so far away."

"Assistance from New Hampshire would be rejected by the court," Randolph pointed out.

"I'm aware of that, but I cannot think of any other option. Any *southern* option."

"I thought as much."

"What about you?" Beede said. "Are there any friends in New Orleans—witnesses, perhaps—who can vouch for your freed status?"

"I had shown my manumission papers to a few people, while I still had them," Randolph admitted. "Unfortunately, they were colored people and their testimony would be discounted. Two of them were slaves, whose testimony would not even be permitted."

"I fear you are right," Beede said. "We are trapped in a paradox; those who are in a position to know the truth are not trusted; those who are trusted do not know. Moreover, they are white men who have a vested interest in perpetuating the slave system."

"There is also the problem of Louisa," Randolph added. "Even if I regain my freedom, she will still be a slave. I shall have to remain here—if I'm not *ordered* to leave Louisiana—to work for her release. It's a discouraging predicament."

It was not, Beede reflected later, a conversation likely to cheer either man.

Although he realized the futility of it, Beede forced himself, during the ensuing week, to call again on every acquaintance from his days in New Orleans in the hope of finding corroboration of Randolph's freedom. But he was retracing his steps from the preceding week, and he learned nothing from the experience. He had friends who would have been happy to assist him, but they had known Randolph only as a slave and could not confirm that he had been freed. And he could see that his acquaintances were tiring of his continued visits.

Before Beede knew it, it was Sunday, the day before court was scheduled to resume. Beede accompanied Dumond to Mass, hoping that the cadences of the ritual might jog some memory that he had misplaced. It did not help.

After Mass, Beede and Dumond went their separate ways. Beede wandered in the direction of Congo Square, where the city's slave population gathered on Sundays to celebrate the brief respite from their labors. He had some hopes that he might see a remembered face from his years in the city, who might lead his search in a more fruitful direction. As slaves, they would not be permitted to testify, but perhaps someone there might remember yet another person—a white man—who could affirm Randolph's status.

He was unsuccessful and finally took to wandering aimlessly through the streets of the old city. Eventually, he took refuge in a tavern, where he commandeered a corner table and drank a considerable quantity of wine, all alone.

It was early evening when Daisy, Pierre Dumond's young servant girl, answered a knock at the door and opened it to see a sight that she could not have imagined. The man who stood before her wore a bottle-green suit of a style that had been out of fashion for many years. It was, in addition, made of wool, and the man who wore it had wilted in the damp, springtime heat. He was none too prepossessing, standing barely five-feet-three in height and measuring, she thought, nearly as wide in girth as he was tall. The gray wisps of hair formed a wilted fringe around his ears, and the perspiration beaded on his pink forehead. Daisy stared in amazement at this strange apparition, forgetting the manners she had been taught.

"Good evening," the man said with a smile. "Have I reached the home of Mr. Dumond? I have urgent business to discuss with him."

"This the right place, yessuh," the girl said. "Only M'sieur Dumond ain't here right now, and I don't know when he might be back."

"Pity," the man said. "Do you know where he might be reached?"

"No, suh, I don't. If you'll wait a minute, I'll ask Betty. He mighta said somethin' to her about when he'll be back for dinner."

She scampered away before he could speak again. After a lengthy wait on the doorstep, she returned with a large, elderly, dark-faced woman wearing an apron and a head scarf.

"You the gentleman askin' about M'sieur Dumond?" the woman said. "I don't 'spect him for hours. He and that M'sieur Beede are down at the Cabildo. You might be able to catch him there."

"Mr. Beede, as well?" the man said. "Excellent. Would you be so kind as to direct me? I'm new to the city, I'm afraid, and I find it difficult to know my way around."

"Oh, you won't have no trouble," the cook said with a smile, and she pointed him in the direction of Rue St. Peter. "You just follow that there street down toward the river, and the Cabildo will come up on your left. Right next door to the cathedral."

"Thank you very much," the man said and turned to go in the direction she had indicated.

"If you miss him and he returns here," the cook called after him, "kin I tell him who's lookin' for him?"

"Oh, certainly, although I doubt the name will mean anything to him. Mr. Beede will recognize it, however. It's Tomkins."

"Tomkins," the cook repeated, rolling the unfamiliar sounds over in her mouth.

"That's correct," the man said. "Tell him that Israel Tomkins came to call."

Chapter 26

Beede had spent the night walking the streets of the old town, seeking witnesses who might shed some light on Randolph's situation. He found none, but he had not expected otherwise. As for Louisa he had, he admitted to himself, given up all hope. She was clearly a slave, and Schneider's confirmation of her "purchase" would not hold up against the testimony of a white man such as Devall. In matters such as this, Beede suspected legality would be subordinated to questions of commerce.

Beede arrived at court the following morning fatigued from lack of sleep and in possession of no more knowledge than he had had the previous day. He was surprised, upon entering the courtroom, to find that Dumond had preceded him. And sitting beside him—

Beede's heart jumped—was a man Beede had not seen for many months.

"Mr. Tomkins," he said, pumping the old man's hand with more emotion than he had anticipated. "I'm extremely happy to see you. I regret to inform you that you have arrived at an inauspicious time. Randolph . . . and I are in dire straits."

"So I'm given to understand," Tomkins said with a curious smile. "If you were not, I should not have undertaken a journey of such magnitude. But if you will call me as a witness, I believe I can be of assistance."

Beede shook his head in sorrow. "I appreciate your intentions, sir, not to mention the determination you have displayed. But you are a Northerner—a Yankee—and the court is not likely to give your testimony much credence."

"What have you to lose?" Tomkins replied. "I believe I may surprise you. I have information that I believe could turn the tables."

Beede turned to Dumond. "You know what he is going to say?"

"In the main. Not all of the particulars."

"Did you put him up to this?"

Dumond shook his head. "I plead guilty to informing him of recent developments and inquiring as to whether there was anything that could be done. That is all."

Beede returned his attention to Tomkins. "Need I inquire as to the substance of your evidence?"

"You may . . . or you may simply proceed in the belief that I mean neither you nor Randolph any harm."

"But surely—" Beede began, just as the door to the courtroom opened and the judge made his entrance.

Tomkins turned aside to take a seat. "Just call me to

the stand and trust me," he said in a low voice as he moved away.

Beede was in a quandary. He did not believe Tomkins would attempt to scuttle Randolph's case. But he had not been present during the earlier hearings—indeed, had never been to the South before. As a magistrate, Tomkins would understand the rules of evidence in a broad sense, but he was not a lawyer. Would his testimony be relevant to the case? If not, Tomkins' presence could only alienate the court.

On the other hand, Beede admitted to himself, Tomkins was smart enough to grasp the essence of the proceedings. More to the point, Tomkins was his only hope.

"Your Honor, with the court's permission I should like to call my first witness,"Beede said.

"Does the plaintiff have any objection?" the judge asked.

"Yes, Your Honor," Harrison said. "It hardly seems necessary to call witnesses. This case is self-evident, or as nearly so as makes no difference. Calling witnesses at this late date seems intended merely to prolong the inevitable."

"Your Honor, I believe the testimony of this witness may alter the outcome of the trial," Beede said, hoping privately that it would be so. "I confess I don't know the substance of his testimony, but he has assured me that he has evidence concerning the status of the man I know as Randolph."

"Why weren't we informed of this at the beginning of the trial?" Harrison said in objection. "Mr. Beede is pulling a rabbit out of his hat."

"Your Honor," Beede said, "I was unaware until a

few minutes ago that my witness was present in the city.
I could not have notified the court until this very morning, as I am now doing."

"Sit down, Jamie," the judge said. "I'll hear the witness."

Grumbling, Harrison returned to his seat. Tomkins
waddled to the stand and took the oath.

"Please state your name and address for the court,"
Beede said.

"Israel S. Tomkins, of Warrensboro, New Hampshire. The 'S' is for Sturdivant."

"Objection! The witness is a Northerner, moreover a
Yankee! Nothing he says can be relevant to this case!"

"I'll be the judge of that, Jamie. Sit down."

"Mr. Tomkins," Beede said, "as opposing counsel
has noted, your home is quite some distance from
Louisiana. Why did you come all this way to testify
here this morning?"

"I felt that I had knowledge that could bear upon the
outcome of this case and prevent a terrible injustice
from being visited upon a good friend."

"I'm not certain I understand," Beede said honestly.
"What sort of information do you have?"

"Well, the question at issue here is whether the man
we call Randolph is slave or free, is it not?" Tomkins
replied. "I have evidence that he is a free man, or more
properly, a freedman. I felt it was my duty to bring this
evidence to the court's attention."

"Very commendable of you, I'm sure," the judge
said dryly. "And so you traveled more than a thousand
miles to bring us your evidence? That is remarkably
conscientious, I must say."

"Mr. Beede and Mr. Randolph are highly respected

members of our community," Tomkins said. "They are known for their integrity and their helpfulness, and we are loath to lose them or see them come to harm. New England communities depend on neighborliness for our prosperity—indeed, for our very survival."

"All very admirable, I'm sure," the judge said. "But do you have any evidence that will be of interest to this court?"

"I believe so, Your Honor. I made several stops, on my journey to New Orleans, specifically for the purpose of gathering such evidence. My first stop was in our state capital, Concord, where I obtained documents attesting to the purchase of land in Warrensboro by Mr. Beede and the later transfer of ownership in an adjacent farmstead to Mr. Randolph. Mr. Randolph inherited his property from a neighbor, Jacob Wolf, now deceased. I can offer these papers in evidence if you wish."

"I would like to see these documents," the judge said.

"I'm aware that slaves cannot own property," Tomkins said as he passed the papers to the bench. "And in any event, slavery is not permitted in New Hampshire. The fact that Mr. Randolph was permitted to take possession of the farm is evidence that he is a free man."

"Perhaps in New Hampshire," the judge said as he leafed through the papers. "Not necessarily in Louisiana."

There was silence in the courtroom as the judge perused the papers. Beede glanced quickly at opposing counsel's table. He saw Devall straining to rise in objection, but Harrison, with his arm around the plaintiff's shoulders, prevented him from moving.

"These seem to be in order," the judge said at last.

"But as you pointed out yourself, slaves cannot own property. What evidence can you provide to show that this boy is *not* a slave?"

"Your Honor, I have in my possession an affidavit from one who has personal knowledge of Randolph's status. He is a Westerner, rather than a southern man, but he is a slaveholder, also."

"That seems more pertinent," the judge said. "Do you have this affidavit on your person?"

"I do."

"And is the court aware of this individual? I cannot take the word of a stranger without corroboration."

"Oh, I feel certain the court has heard of the man before," Tomkins said with a poorly concealed smirk. "His name is Andrew Jackson and, until recently, he was president of the United States."

Chapter 27

"**A**pproach the bench," the judge said, motioning to Beede and Harrison.

"Your Honor, I must object," Harrison said almost immediately after arriving at the bench. "General Jackson is not here and cannot attest to the authenticity of this document. This tactic has the smell of desperation all about it."

"Mr. Beede?"

"Your Honor, I was unaware of Mr. Tomkins's efforts on our behalf, but I do not doubt his information. When I worked with President Jackson I spoke with him about my intentions concerning Randolph, and he witnessed the signing of the papers of manumission. I confess that I had forgotten that he had been a witness when I freed Randolph."

*

"I will see this affidavit," the judge said. "Mr. Tomkins, is this paper in your possession?"

"It is," Tomkins said. He produced a document from an inside pocket of his coat and handed it to the judge.

"Your Honor, I request a ruling," Harrison said. "Mr. Beede has produced this document out of thin air, as it were. Clearly it is another attempt by counsel to subvert the cause of justice. You cannot give it any weight."

"I'll be the judge of that, Jamie," the judge said. "Judging is my job, not yours."

He gave the papers a quick look before turning to the attorneys who faced him.

"This will require some time," he said. "Court will be in recess until two o'clock this afternoon."

Harrison accosted Beede on the street as he, Dumond, and Tomkins left the Cabildo.

"What are you up to, Beede?" he said. "You can't hope to get away with this!"

"I am not trying to 'get away'—as you put it—with anything," Beede said heatedly. "Randolph was my slave, and I freed him. Therefore, he is a free man, regardless of the claims of your client, and I intend to see that he stays that way."

"You intend to persist in this deception?"

"No deception is intended. I merely speak the truth."

Harrison hacked and spit tobacco juice on the street.

"I've never heard of this 'Randolph' person, but my client assures me that the man in question is a slave named Toby. I've no desire to humiliate a fellow lawyer, but I will do whatever is necessary to protect my client from calumny and falsehood. Let this be a warning to you. You proceed at your own peril."

He spit again. The juice spattered near Beede's foot, splashing on his pant leg, before he strode away.

Beede and his companions stared after the retreating man.

"That was strange," Tomkins said at last.

"Indeed."

"He certainly seems convinced that Randolph belongs to him. If I didn't know your man, I might be persuaded myself. Do you suppose Randolph has a brother or cousin—a close relative—for whom he might be mistaken?"

"It's possible, I suppose."

"But you think not."

"I don't think it's a simple case of mistaken identity. I think Devall and Harrison have something else in mind."

"And what is that?" Dumond asked.

Beede shrugged.

"That is something I can't fathom," he said. "But for some reason, our adversaries want Randolph out of the way."

"Lucy!"

"I hears you. Keep your voice down. We ain't even s'pose to be talkin'."

"Well, come on over here closer to the wall, then, so I don't have to talk so loud."

Louisa heard Lucy shuffle closer and closer until she bumped against the wall of the cell. It took her an uncommonly long time to make the journey, which was accompanied by a low-pitched clanking sound.

"All right," Lucy said. "Now what you want?"

"Lucy! You in chains?"

"Yep. Ain't you?"

"No, they din't put me in chains! 'Course they don't let me outta this cell, nuther. Maybe they figger they don't need to chain me, long as I don't leave here."

She heard Lucy sit down—hard, from the sound of it—on the floor of her cell.

"Come to think on it, I *din't* see you out front this morning, showin' your stuff," Lucy said. The chains rattled and clanked with every movement of her body. "I wonder why they ain't haulin' you out there so's the buyers can have a look at you. You so pretty, you'd be snapped up real fast-like."

"I don't think they *can* put me out there," Louisa said. "On account of they don't know who owns me. Ol' Miz Hawkins bein' dead, they gots to find out if there's a will somewhere. An' if they *is* a will, it prob'ly says who gets the slaves. They cain't sell me till they knows who *owns* me."

Chapter 28

"I am persuaded," said the judge the next morning, "that Mr. Beede is telling the truth and that the boy he calls Randolph is, indeed, a freedman. Consequently, I order his release from custody."

"Your Honor!" Harrison's protest was almost a whine.

"Quiet, Jamie," the judge said. "You made a strong argument, but you were overwhelmed by the evidence. Return to your table."

The judge now turned to Beede.

"My decision does not, however, resolve the issue of the girl Louisa," he said. "In the absence of opposition, or evidence that she does not belong to M'sieur Devall, I'm compelled to award the girl to M'sieur Devall. Do you have an objection, Mr. Beede?"

"Only, Your Honor, that she and Mr. Randolph were

married some years ago. It doesn't seem right that a man and his wife should be forcibly separated, particularly after Randolph has gone to such lengths to recover her."

"Your Honor!" This from opposing counsel.

"Never mind, Jamie," said the judge. "I'm aware of your interest in this."

Back to Beede.

"And I'm sure you're aware, Mr. Beede, that this alleged marriage, even if true, has no standing in this court or, indeed, under Louisiana law," the judge said. "By your own admission, they were both slaves at the time and were, therefore, not eligible for marriage. Whatever relationship they may have had, it must cede precedence to the prerogatives of the property owner."

"Will you not take this marriage into consideration?" Beede asked in desperation.

"I am not permitted to do so," the judge replied. "Unless you have further evidence, I'm obliged to return possession of the girl to M'sieur Devall."

"I have no additional evidence, I fear."

The judge nodded. "Then I must rule—"

"However," Beede said, "Mr. Randolph *is* prepared to buy her at a price to be mutually agreed upon. As a free man, he is legally entitled to own slaves, and Louisa is the slave he wants. Will M'sieur Devall name a price for her?"

"That, sir, is between you and M'sieur Devall and is not a proper matter for this court. You may take it up with him directly once court is adjourned."

He gaveled the court to adjournment, and the meager crowd poured out of the room. As the courtroom emptied, Beede approached his adversaries.

"May we meet to discuss Louisa?" he said.

"That is a matter for M'sieur Devall," Harnson said, deferring to his client.

"Certainly," said Devall. "I should happy to meet with Mr. Beede and ... *Mr.* Randolph to discuss the matter. I shall hear your offer in its entirety before I reject it."

"Thank you."

"But make no mistake, sir. I *will* reject it."

"You haven't heard our offer yet."

"No matter. I will reject it."

"We're prepared to be generous."

"I should hope so. That will make my rejection all the sweeter. Please do, sir. Make an offer. Make it a high one. I shall consider it honestly, and then I shall turn you down."

"Then you do not intend to sell her?"

"On the contrary, sir, I do fully intend to sell her. But not to you. I have in mind a small sugar plantation downstream from Twin Oaks. The planter, a M'sieur Prudhomme, finds it difficult to obtain slaves and keep them, for they have an unfortunate tendency to die in his cane fields."

He tipped his hat to Beede and sauntered out into the hallway, leaving Beede to stare after him in anger and confusion.

R andolph was released that evening and returned to Dumond's residence. He immediately sought out Beede.

"I have news," Randolph said. "I don't know what it means, but it's interesting."

"What is it?"

"Lucy is in the jail."

"Who is Lucy?"

"She was a runaway like Louisa. Louisa met her at the runaway camp in the swamp."

"She was captured, you mean?"

"That's right. And she says Jasper caused it to happen! She has an interesting story, according to Louisa. Perhaps you should hear it."

"Sure it was Jasper set me up! Couldna been nobody else!"

Lucy, Beede saw, was still steaming about her treatment. She paced from one side of her cell to the other, swinging her arms from side to side as if pulled by strings, stopping now and then as if to gather strength for another outburst.

"How did he set you up, as you put it?" Beede asked.

"He sent me out from the camp on a wild goose chase," she said. "And while I was out, he called the pattyrollers on me. I dint have no chance."

"How can you be sure he called them?" Beede asked. "Don't the patrols check that area now and again? Perhaps they simply came across your trail during the course of your wanderings."

"One of them big white men called me by name," Lucy said. "He dint have no reason to know my name, less somebody told him and tell what I look like. No, he knowed who I was just as soon as he saw me."

"Why would this Jasper fellow do something like that?"

"Money, I 'spects. Jasper likes money a awful lot."

"But what good would the money do? He's a slave. He can't spend it without attracting attention. And what slave would trust him after such an act?"

"Slaves what don't know what he done, that's who," she said. "So many new ones every day, they don't get the word till it's too late."

"It's just conceivable that he *could* get away with it," Randolph said. "As she said, there are new slaves every day. You can see the coffles streaming into the markets all day long. Some of them are going to try an escape, and anyone who makes it to the swamps is likely to run into Jasper and his men."

"I can see that," Beede said. "I can't see how he gains from it, however."

"Nor do I, offhand," Randolph said. "But I can't see him doing this for his own amusement. Something's afoot."

"Then we had better learn what it is," Beede said. "And we had probably better learn quickly."

They left the slave market together and walked up Rue Royale in the direction of Canal Street.

"I would feel more comfortable," Randolph said, "if we could remove Louisa from this situation. There are forces at work here that I do not understand, and I fear for her safety."

"As do I," said Beede. "Though I don't know what we can do to protect her, under the circumstances."

"I've been thinking," Randolph said. "It might be worthwhile to put the slave market under observation for a few days. It's possible that Jasper and his followers have future plans for Lucy, and perhaps for Louisa as well."

"You may be right," Beede said. "Perhaps we should

work in shifts for the next few days. We can join the
others nearby and watch for Jasper to show up. He'll
not trust this business to an underling."

Conrad Schneider suspected that his deputy's
house was empty long before it came in sight. He
could smell no smoke. It was still too cool to go without at least a small fire on the hearth, but no smoke,
however faint, emanated from Howie's chimney.

His deputy had gone away again? Where had he
gone, and why hadn't he said he was going?

The front door was locked. Schneider walked around
the building, peering into all the windows he could
reach, but there was no sign of life. It was not as if
Howie had moved away—all his possessions seemed
intact and unmolested—but the occupants had gone and
had left no notice.

What about George?

The blacksmith's shop where the slave worked also
was unoccupied. The fire had been banked but not permitted to die out. Schneider reached his fingers into the
water bath and sprinkled drops on the coals. There was,
as he had surmised, a sudden eruption of rising steam,
faint but unmistakable. The fire probably had been
banked for several days, but it would be only the work
of a minute or two to bring it back to life.

So. George gone. Howie gone. Miz Howie (Schneider could never remember her name) gone as well. And
yet, gone with no sense of permanence. They had left
their possessions behind; clearly they intended to return, and soon. Howie and the missus, at least; it always

was hard to tell about slaves, for they had so few possessions.

George had no cabin of his own, but a makeshift bed lay in the corner of the blacksmith's shop. Schneider poked at it with a stick and felt something hard under the straw. Moving the straw and the pallet aside, he discovered a small, crude tin box placed snugly in a hollow in the dirt floor.

He picked up the box. It was surprisingly heavy for such a small object. He estimated that the box was large enough to hold a handful of stones, or marbles. Perhaps flint and steel for making fire. But it was too heavy for flint and steel.

The lid was secured by a length of wire that been fused end to end. Schneider deliberated for only a few moments before retrieving a pair of pliers from the hearth and snipping the wire in two. George was a slave; he was not entitled to privacy.

As he had suspected, the box contained coins, and they were identical to the coins Schneider had discovered earlier: golden half eagles, rather crudely molded but essentially identical to mint products in other respects. He picked up a few, hefted them in his hands, and discovered that they were heavy enough to pass as the real thing.

There were fifty coins in the box; not a fortune except, perhaps, to a slave, but a sizable sum even by white men's standards. It was enough to buy a significant quantity of tobacco, or sugar, or rum. A few acres of land. An inexpensive slave.

Perhaps George was acquiring coins to buy his freedom? But no slave could afford to flaunt such a sum in cash without causing suspicion. Particularly not in gold.

What, then, would be the purpose of acquiring such a sum in such a form?

Money, Schneider thought, was not sought after for aesthetic reasons; its value lay in its utility. George could not realize the value of his little hoard in any open marketplace, where his possession of it would inspire suspicion and scrutiny. His plans, therefore, must involve one of those commercial venues where little regard was paid to questions of legality.

There were a few of those that he could think of: contraband of one sort or another; slaves imported illegally from Africa or the Caribbean; absinthe, which was now illegal but was still highly popular in some circles. . . .

Slaves, he thought, was the most likely answer. Since 1808 it had been illegal to import new slaves into the United States, which meant that the South had to deal with its labor needs in some other way. One way, of course, was slaves from other planters in other states where the slave population had outpaced its usefulness. Another was to defy the law and smuggle slaves into the country.

The need for laborers was especially acute in the sugar fields. It was a short and brutish life that awaited those men and women who were relegated to the cane fields; heat, humidity, disease, and backbreaking labor—often spiced with the touch of the whip—was their inevitable lot. A man who had access to such a labor force could name his own price for his "merchandise."

Had George, a loyal slave who would speak no ill of his masters, been suddenly transformed into George, a dealer in other slaves? If so, he could not do so alone;

he would require an accomplice—a white accomplice—who could deal in the slave markets on an equal basis with other brokers.

Had he an accomplice and was he actually engaged in the slave trade? Schneider thought it might be worthwhile to find out. He decided to return to his boardinghouse, where he would stock up with food for a long night of watching and waiting.

Beede, in the meantime, was doing much the same, and Randolph insisted on going with him.

"This matter affects me," Randolph pointed out as the two of them packed food for the undertaking. "But for you and Mr. Tomkins, I could have been sold back into slavery, to end my life in the cane fields. And as for Louisa, this man Devall—whoever he may be—is a stumbling block to her freedom. If something has gone wrong, I want to know about it."

"I can't dispute that," Beede said. "And it is certainly possible that I may need your assistance, but please stay with me. If we are separated, there is no way to tell what might happen."

"I'll stay close," Randolph said. "The cane fields hold no attraction for me."

Upon reaching the market they found a dry spot behind a rain barrel and settled down to wait for darkness. This area of the city had not been blessed with streetlights, as had those blocks closer to Canal Street. If they remained without moving, they should be as nearly invisible as human beings could be.

It was raining, of course, as was often the case in early spring, but that was a good thing, for it meant that there was no illumination from the moon to give away their location.

But it made no difference, for no one approached the slave market all night. Beede and Randolph trudged wearily back to Dumond's wineshop in the gray light of the predawn.

Unknown to Beede, Schneider's experience was the same. He waited in the darkness near the blacksmith shop until just before dawn, but the little shack was as empty in the morning as it had been the previous day. Schneider wondered briefly if he had misinterpreted the signs he had seen, or if he had been recognized in his hiding place and George had been scared off. Schneider concluded eventually that he would continue to keep watch for another night, or perhaps two, in the hope of intercepting George's return, or Howie's. In the final analysis, Schneider thought, he had nothing better to do at present than to await developments—whatever they might be.

George returned to the blacksmith shed not long after midnight the next day. Schneider had almost fallen asleep when he heard the grating of metal on metal and glanced up from his hiding place to see a shadowed form working the latch on the shop door—a form he recognized instantly as George's. As he watched, George opened the lock and slipped through the opening. A minute later, Schneider saw a spark, and the slave's face was momentarily lit through the window in the darkness as he applied a burning brand to the wick of a hurricane lantern.

When the lantern was lit, George kicked the door

shut, and Schneider heard him rummaging in the shop. A moment or two later, Schneider heard George humming tunelessly to himself.

Schneider moved quietly toward the building and took up a position beneath an open window. The window was on the opposite side of the shop from the forge, and Schneider thought he might not be seen if he were to raise himself to peer into the shop.

He did so and was astonished at the sight.

George was melting something in a small crucible. Laid alongside him was a small stack of gold coins. Nearby, Schneider saw, was a mold. As he watched, George poured the liquefied contents of the crucible into the waiting mold. Then he set the mold aside and dropped another coin into the crucible. He reached for a poker lying nearby and began to poke the now-dormant coals, which produced a feeble flame.

Schneider decided he had seen enough. He slipped away from the window and made for the door. Opening it swiftly and noisily, he caught the slave by surprise in the act of melting a coin.

"I'll take that," he said.

George complied wordlessly, handing Schneider the poker. Schneider threw it across the shop, where it landed near a stack of firewood. The wood, fortunately, did not catch fire, for the poker was cooling quickly.

"I see you have yourself a little cottage industry goin' here," Schneider said. "Does Howie know about this?"

George laughed. "Who do you think made this mold? It ain't nothin' I could do. I'm just usin' it a little when he ain't around and don't know I'm usin' it."

"Where'd you get the coins? They from Howie, too?"

"Yessah. But I don't know where he got them, and he don't know I found them. I just squirrels them away, a few at a time, in this hidin' place I got, and he don't even I know they're missin'."

"Sounds mighty convenient," Schneider said. "But I'm going to have to relieve you of these coins until I can find out who they belong to. That goes for the ones you tucked away in your little box, too."

"You know about them? Damn, Sheriff, that ain't fair!"

"I'm not a fair guy. Dig 'em up, George, or I'll do it for you. I know where they are."

George did so reluctantly. When he handed the coins to the sheriff, Schneider tied the slave's hands and led him away.

"Where you takin' me?" George asked petulantly.

"I think I'll tuck you out of the way for a little while," Schneider said. "That way we can have ourselves a nice little chat or two."

"I'll be back in a little bit," Schneider told him. "Then we'll have that little talk." He led the slave to the smokehouse, barred the door behind him and left to forage for something to eat. He returned after a couple of hours, hunger slaked and a sense of well-being pervading. He found the slave rather the worse for wear. George, Schneider suspected, was not accustomed to missing meals.

"I think it's time now for our discussion, George," Schneider said on entering the cell.

"I'se awful hungry, Sheriff Schneider, sir."

"I'm counting on it," Schneider said. "Do you think

we might hold a more interesting conversation if you were fed?"

"Oh, yes, sir. I feel most definitely so, sir."

"Well, we'll have to see to that, I suppose. But first we'll talk."

"Been a long time since I et, sir."

"Could be a long time before you eat again, 'less I get some answers," Schneider said. "Somethin' is goin' on around here, and I believe you're in the thick of it."

"Don't know what you mean, sir."

"Then I guess you're not hungry enough," Schneider said as he turned to go. "I'll see you in the morning."

"Wait!"

Schneider turned back.

"What you want to know?"

"That's better," Schneider said. "For starters, tell me about these coins."

"I dint steal them, sir. I'se tellin' the truth!"

"Didn't think you did, George. But I do want to know where they came from—and how you got them. Who gave them to you?"

George abruptly abandoned his abject demeanor and straightened to his full height.

"Nobody done give 'em to me," he said with a haughty air that bordered on smugness. "I made them myself."

"I know that. But where'd they come from? You don't have a gold mine or a smelter that we don't know about, do you?"

"No, sir. Massa Howie's got a stash of them. Don't know where he got 'em but they sure is a lot of them."

"Just like these?"

"Well, they got different pictures on them. I just puts

them in this mold, here, and they come out lookin' the
way you see them. 'Course, I melts them down, first, so
they're runny."

"I'd like to see one of them before you melt it,"
Schneider said. "I want to see what they look like in
their original form."

"Yes, sir. I'll have to leave the shop for a minute."

"I'll go with you."

George led Schneider to a cleared space back behind
the main house. George brushed away underbrush to
uncover a spot where, it was clear, digging had gone on
recently. The dirt that covered the hole was removed
easily, and a tin box similar to the one Schneider had
seen before appeared.

Schneider took the box from George and shook it.
The box was heavier than it looked, and he could hear
the metallic clanking of coins. It was sealed like the first
box, with a bit of wire. He returned with George to the
blacksmith shop, where he snipped the wire.

Sovereigns. British gold coins. Schneider counted
thirty. From their weight, Schneider estimated, they
would total . . . he wasn't certain, but he thought they
would be worth perhaps a hundred and fifty dollars.

"Is this all of it?" he asked.

George shrugged. "I don' know," he said. "I think
Massa Howie might be refillin' it now and again."

"Doesn't he keep track? Won't he know when
you've taken some?"

"I don' think Massa Howie counts too good,"
George replied. "Tell the truth, I don' know that he
cares too much, long as there's enough for what he
wants to do."

"And what does he want to do?"

"I don't know for certain," George said. "I think with some of it he wants to buy me. I'm just on loan, like. And maybe a few more. I think he likes the idea of having a whole buncha slaves."

"And what do *you* want to do with these coins?" Schneider said.

George grinned and spread his hands. "Same as Massa Howie," he said. "I wants to buy me, too."

Chapter 29

Beede and Randolph spent several hours in hiding, during which time Beede reflected that springtime could be painfully cold, even in Louisiana.

When the move they had been waiting for was finally made, it came not at night but in the early morning, about an hour before dawn, and it was not Jasper who made it. As a consequence, Beede almost missed the import of it all.

"Someone's coming!" Randolph's whisper was almost too soft for Beede to hear, but it was followed by a nudge in the ribs that brought Beede up from the well of sleep into which he had fallen.

There was a moon tonight, and Beede saw at once what Randolph had seen.

"Is that not . . . ?"

"Yes," said Beede. "I met him again recently, on the

quay. His name is Prescott, and he says he's a cotton factor from Memphis."

"Do you have reason to doubt this claim?"

"None whatsoever."

"Still, it's strange," said Randolph. "What can he be doing at a slave market many hours before it opens for business?"

"Let us see if we can determine that," Beede said. He slipped away from the shadow in which they had been hiding and crossed the street to the slave market while Prescott entered the building, his back to Beede and Randolph.

They strained in vain to hear the conversation going on inside. They were startled when the doorknob began turning and Prescott appeared at the threshold once more, accompanied this time by the slave woman known as Lucy.

"Mr. Beede!" Prescott said in obvious astonishment. "I did not expect to see you, of all people, at a slave market, least of all at this hour."

"I might say the same of you, sir," Beede replied. "I suppose I should not be surprised that a southern white man might buy a colored woman, probably for his own amusement. I can say, however, that it does you no credit."

To which Prescott burst into laughter.

"*Buy* her?" he said when his laughter subsided. "I did indeed *buy* her! But not for the purpose you seem to suspect."

"You are removing this young woman from a slave market, in the dark of night. Are you saying I should disbelieve the evidence of my own eyes?"

"No, sir. I ask merely that you not believe everything you see until you understand its import. I'm not buying this young woman for servitude. On the contrary, I am freeing her!"

Chapter 30

"I would have thought that you, of all people, would have understood what I was about," Prescott said. They were back at Dumond's house on Rue Royale an hour later, sipping the good, strong coffee that Dumond's cook invariably offered to visitors.

"I do *not* understand," Beede said, "but I would like to. Please explain it to me."

Prescott let out a heavy sigh and sipped once more from his coffee.

"Very well," he said. "I am a Quaker."

"A Quaker?"

"I belong to the Society of Friends, yes, and I, like most of my brethren, am fervently opposed to slavery. And before you ask it, yes, it *is* an unusual moral position for one such as I, who has lived his entire life in the South. Nevertheless, I consider slavery to be one of the world's greatest scourges, and I am committed to doing my best to stop it, as are many others of my acquaintance."

"You are a cotton factor," Beede said. "You told me so yourself."

"Quite so. And my livelihood depends on cotton production, which is generated almost entirely by slave labor. I'm aware of the disparity between my principles and my vocation, but there you have it. It's difficult for me to reconcile these two elements of my character, but I feel certain that a way can be found to produce cotton for the northern mills without destroying human beings along the way."

"And so you steal slaves from dealers?"

"I *buy* slaves from dealers," Prescott said. "I take them with me on my journeys until I find an opportunity to get them to freedom. Usually that means I take them with me into one of the border states, where I can find sympathetic people—other Quakers, as a rule— who will see to it that they reach safety. I can rescue only a few, I fear, for my funds are not without limit, but I take advantage of opportunities when they arise."

"Where do you obtain your funds for such purposes?" Beede asked.

"There are others, like-minded to myself, who contribute to the cause," he said. "In this instance, however, I received an unexpected bequest—and from a slave, no less."

"A bequest?"

"A bagful of gold coins, to be precise. I was instructed to use the coins to purchase the freedom of as many slaves as I could buy. Since this corresponded to my own inclinations, I did so without hesitation."

"And how do you determine whom to buy?" Randolph said. "My wife is being held at that market, and I would have you buy her. I can compensate you for your expenditures."

"Louisa, you mean? Yes, I met her through Lucy and would have bought her as well, but the trader would not part with her. Some question of ownership, apparently. I'm sorry that I cannot help you, but I dare not return too frequently to the same dealer—and in this case it would make no difference. It was clear he would not sell her."

"I am determined to free her," said Randolph. "If necessary, I will acquire a gun and break her out by force."

"That would be dangerous, indeed, for both of you," said Prescott. "And you could not get far before you are captured. This is just desperation speaking."

"Perhaps Lucy could be of assistance in this case," Beede said. "She knows the inner workings of the slave market firsthand."

Lucy was sent for. She had been housed in the kitchen with Betty, Dumond's cook, who had pressed her into service to help with meal preparations.

"We shared a cell," Lucy said. "These past few days, so many slaves arrived that we was crowded in together. I was moved from my cell to Louisa's."

"I want to free her," Randolph said. "I'm prepared to use force if necessary, but I would rather not. Obviously, it increases the risk."

Lucy thought.

"Don't see how you can do it," she said after a moment. "The cells is crowded now. Ain't no way to free her without everybody knowin' about it—and they ain't goin' to want to sit quiet while you frees somebody else."

"Then we should find a way to separate her from her cellmates," Beede said. "Moreover, it must be something that will not raise danger signals. It wouldn't be practical to free everybody."

"I wonder why she hasn't been sold already," said Randolph. "She would bring a good price, I think, and yet she has been held out of the general trading."

"I was told that she was spoken for," said Prescott. "They're talking about the need to establish ownership, but I don't think that's the real reason she hasn't been sold. The owner is someone known to the trader, who wants above all else to sell her down the river. He's apparently prepared to forgo all better offers to do so. It's my understanding that his prospective buyer will be arriving by boat tomorrow."

"That sounds like spite," said Beede. "I wish I knew why Devall was doing this. It may be just because of the trial, but somehow I feel there must be more to it than that, however. Devall has been adversarial from the beginning."

"It requires very little incentive to mistreat a slave," Randolph said. "Slaves are beaten, or sold, for minor infractions real or imagined."

"She really hasn't been in Louisiana long enough to inspire hatred," Beede said. "As late as last November she was living in Virginia. Aside from two weeks on the road to New Orleans and a week on the trading floor, she's been living at the Hawkins plantation, which is about as isolated as a place can be."

"She was with Jasper and us for a week," Lucy pointed out. "And Jasper is somebody you don't wanna cross. I don't know that she ran afoul of Jasper, but it wouldna been hard to do."

"It sounds more like spite directed at you, Mr. Beede," Prescott said. "Or to Randolph, or perhaps the both of you."

"I don't think it matters whether she offended Jasper or not, or if it's all Devall's doing," Randolph said. "The task before us is to persuade the slave dealer who now has her to give her up. Somehow we must hit on a measure that makes it appear to his advantage to let her go. It should be something that persuades him he would be better off without her in the slave pens. Moreover, it should, ideally, be something that will not cause him to have second thoughts later."

"And do you have a plan that might accomplish this?"

"Why, yes," Randolph said. "Now that you mention it, I believe I do. I'll need assistance, of course, and Sheriff Schneider would fill the bill perfectly."

Louisa was alone in her cell again and, even more than before, the fear and loneliness overwhelmed her. She had been frightened before, but she had always managed to seize on an element of hope. Even after Randolph had been taken from her, ostensibly to be freed, she had clung to the belief that he would return and free her—how, she did not know.

But it had been a week now, and no one had come, and belief was coming harder every day. Now, in the postmidnight darkness, she shivered and tried not to fall victim to self-pity. It was hard not to feel sorry for herself whenever she thought about her future. She had heard stories of life on the sugar plantations, and they filled her with terror.

She had not considered the possibility of escape. Perhaps she should do so now.

But what possibility was there? Reluctantly, she considered, there was none. She could not scale these walls, even if she were not watched constantly. Neither could she hope to overpower a guard, or deceive one.

Perhaps she could suborn a guard, or tempt one with her body. Men had always been attracted to her; perhaps she could use that to her advantage. But what man would believe that she would have the boldness to follow through on her offer, or indeed the opportunity?

She could think of no other options, and she slumped forward on the verge of despair.

She heard a noise in the adjacent cell.

"Hey!" said a woman's voice.

"Lucy?"

"Nah, I ain't Lucy," the voice replied. "My name's Dicey. Is you Louisa?"

"I don't know no Dicey."

The other woman laughed. "No, and I don't know you, nuther, but I heard about you, all right."

"You heard about *me?* How'd you hear about me?"

"In the showroom. I was doin' my stuff for the buyers when this white man comes up to me and tol' me a message for you."

"For me?"

"Ain't that just what I said? For you, yes."

"Who was this white man?"

"I don't know. I tol' you he just comes up to me and ax if I knows you. An' I say no, an' he says, 'Well, you git to know her, and when you do, give her a message from me.' And I say, 'Who *are* you?'"

"What did he say?"

"He didn't tell me his name, I tol' you already. He just say, she'll know."

"How am I going to know if he dint tell you?"

"I don't know. Tha's just what he say."

"All right," Louisa said. "What's the message?"

"He say he be comin' sometime in the next few days—he don' know zactly when. And when you sees him you needs to play along with whatever he do."

"That's all?"

"All he say to me."

Louisa thought. "What's this white man look like?"

"Thought you'd ask me that. He was kinda tall. Had a lot of greasy hair, when he took his hat off, and a great big red nose. Talked a little like a Kaintuck, you know? Kinda slow and twangy."

The description sounded like someone she had met, and met recently, but she could not remember where or when.

"Think he was tellin' it straight?" Louisa asked. "He weren't settin' me up for somethin'?"

"I don' know," Dicey said. "You gon' have to be the judge of that. When you see him."

What did it mean? Louisa wondered. Salvation and freedom? Or just a new owner with lustful ideas? Louisa thought it over without reaching a conclusion until, against her will, she slept.

Chapter 31

Argus Prudhomme had not wanted to make this trip upriver, for a variety of reasons, but he felt an obligation to his friend. The girl was being held in a cell at one of the downtown slave markets, and the dealer had been instructed to give Prudhomme first option on her—as if he wanted her! He had quite enough slaves already and probably more than he could really afford. She was reputedly an excellent cook, but he had a cook already. And this girl was from Virginia, and if the rumors were true, cooks in the North did not know their seasonings. Garlic, in particular, seemed to be anathema to them.

But his friend had said that the girl was pretty, a fancy, and he could use that. His wife had died of the yellow fever nearly ten years ago, and he missed her vigor and enthusiasm in bed. He had been reluctant to seek a replacement; few women came to the Barataria of their own accord, and fewer still would be willing to stay in that isolated place. At one time he'd made an occasional journey to New Orleans to sample the wares of the brothels, but he had gradually given it up. It was too long a trip, requiring at least an overnight stay, and he was dependent on the steamboat schedules. The older he grew, the more difficult the journey became.

For the same reason, he was reluctant to seek a wife. It had been so long that he doubted he could perform to the satisfaction of a woman. A slave might be the answer, then, if she were attractive enough and obliging. A slave would not laugh at him or be rude to him, and she might—who knew?—even grow to like him.

And so here he was, standing anxiously at the railing, watching the green riverbank passing by, wondering what the girl might be like. This business of gratifying a man's desires—no, his needs—was far more difficult than it ought to be, he thought. Such a simple thing should be simple to provide, but there were all those *human* considerations that had to be dealt with.

A flag was flying on the far bank, the signal that a passenger was waiting at the landing, and the boat began the laborious process of backing its stern wheel to move in toward the shore for its passenger. A man was standing on the dock, a small carpetbag on the plank beside him. He was a tall man, with regular features, but even from this distance Prudhomme was struck by the huge, reddish nose that bulged like a promontory from his face.

With a loud discharge of steam, the boat came to rest at the landing, its boiler hissing, stern wheel at rest. The man on the dock snatched his satchel in one hand and swung himself aboard. He nodded briefly to Prudhomme as the boat began making its way out into the channel.

"Evenin'," the newcomer said. Prudhomme returned the nod shortly, neither inviting conversation nor discouraging it. One never knew how to take these Kaintucks—he certainly was no Creole—who might respond to a congenial overture as if it were a proffer of unsolicited companionship. But the new arrival, to Prudhomme's relief, took no more notice of him and, in fact, moved midway toward the stern of the boat, where he removed a packet from inside his coat and began studying it intently.

After a while Prudomme found himself curious about the packet the newcomer was perusing so carefully. Prudhomme was too far away to make much of it, so he moved closer until he was standing only a few feet away. The packet, he realized, was a series of notes for slave buyers. It appeared to contain a description of slaves offered for sale at the very market where Prudhomme was himself bound.

"In the market?" Prudhomme asked casually.

"For servants?" the man said in response. It was a rhetorical question, and they both knew it.

"I'm gonna look, I guess," the man said, answering his own question. "Whether I buy depends on what I see. I need a good carpenter, and someone to work with horses. Fellow I had got himself kicked by a mule, and he won't be no good to me for a month or two."

Prudhomme considered this. Here, he thought, was a man who knew something about the slave market and, for that matter, about purchasing slaves.

"Ever had any experience selecting women?" he asked.

"A little," the man said. "A housemaid or two. I bought myself a nice, fancy piece a few months back, and she's working out very well. That's not something a man can do every day, of course. They're too expensive."

"And you never know if they're going to work out," Prudhomme said. "What if you don't hit it off?"

"Well, I'd say that's her problem, not yours," the man replied with a grin. "It ain't like she has a choice in the matter. Mostly, they'll see the advantages of gettin' on your good side."

"I suppose so," Prudhomme said.

The two men stood in silence as the riverboat continued to churn its way upstream. Prudhomme was beginning to feel more comfortable with the idea of purchasing a woman as a companion. It was true, he thought, that he would hold the upper hand in any relationship with a slave girl. He was, after all, the master. His fears subsided a bit.

"You checked her out, I suppose," the man was saying, breaking into Prudhomme's thoughts.

"Pardon?"

"This fancy piece you're thinkin' about. You checked her out, and she's what she's been ballyhooed to be? You want to check her out before you put down your money and take her home."

"I've not seen the girl, myself," Prudhomme said. "She's been described to me as exceedingly handsome and an excellent cook. What more should I know? As you pointed out, she can hardly refuse me anything I ask."

"Weren't thinking about that. I expect she'll be bid-dable enough."

"Then what?"

"Well," the man said, "how's her health? I once bought a girl with the consumption. I was young at the time and didn't know what to look for, I guess. At any rate, she died on me not more than three months after I bought her. Damn waste of money."

"Consumption, you say. I'll have to look for that."

"Feel her titties. Sometimes when they got the consumption their titties just dry up and wither away. The dealer will stuff paper under their dresses to fill them out a little. Only way to tell is to feel them."

"I'll remember that. Thank you."

"And look out for old Bronze John, too. It's a little early in the season, I grant you, but the yellow fever can sneak up on you. If she's throwin' up that black vomit, of course, you'll know to stay away from her, but the signs might not be as obvious as all that."

"I hadn't thought of that. Clearly, you've had much more experience than I."

The man shrugged. "Been an overseer for ten years now, and my employer seems to trust my judgment. Ain't much I haven't seen. You'll be all right, though. Just remember, when you're conducting a business transaction with a slave dealer, be sure to keep one hand on your purse all the time."

Silence again. Finally Prudhomme said, "If you are going to the market today, might I prevail on you to ac-company me? I must settle some business first at my hotel, but it would be helpful to have the benefit of your insights when I visit the girl." He relayed the description of the girl that he had been given.

The man nodded slowly. "I'm going straight to the market, myself, so I'll be there, before you, most likely. Just look around for me when you arrive."

"What name should I ask for?"

"You'll probably see me around. If you don't, just ask for Nathan. Nathan Bigelow."

Prudhomme nodded in gratitude and returned to the rail, where he sought the city's skyline with renewed eagerness. Perhaps his fortunes were about to change, he thought. The intricacies of the slave market had always left him confused and uncomfortable, but now he had an expert to rely on.

The man was American, of course, and possessed of all the coarse vulgarity of his breed. He'd most likely be inclined to treat a slave in a manner that a Creole would not consider acceptable. On the other hand, the American would be less tolerant of faults that a Creole such as he might overlook. He might notice things that Prudhomme himself would miss, and that would be all to the good.

And, Prudhomme told himself, he would not be required to take the American's advice if, for some reason, he found it inadequate or inappropriate. Meanwhile, he would hang on all the stranger's words and consider them seriously.

Chapter 32

The man calling himself Bigelow arrived at the slave market about an hour later. He called on the dealer and made arrangements to visit personally with some of the livestock. Although Louisa's name was not on the list he gave to the dealer, Bigelow found it easy enough to stray from his announced itinerary and to wander freely among the cells. He found Louisa with little trouble, and they spent quite some time in a low-voiced conversation. Some of the other slaves noted that Louisa's countenance grew more animated during the course of the conversation, and she pressed closer to the bars as if to talk more intimately with the man. Bigelow leaned in, also, and seemed to dab at her face with a stick.

"Remember what I said," Bigelow finally said. After dabbing at her face one more time, he straightened up and walked away, leaving other denizens of the slave pens bursting with unanswered curiosity.

Prudhomme arrived about an hour later and went searching for his new companion. He found the man in the showroom as promised, and the two of them strolled back to the slave cells.

"Well?" Prudhomme forced himself to restrain his eagerness. "You've seen her now. What do you think?"

"She's very pretty," the man called Bigelow said with what Prudhomme felt was a touch of reluctance. "Just as you were told."

"So you think she's a good buy? I should go ahead?"

"I don't recall telling you I'd make a buy recommendation, did I? This'll have to be your own decision. I don't want to have you holding it against me if you're unhappy with your decision later."

"Is there a problem here?" Prudhomme said worriedly. "You did say you'd let me know your opinion, didn't you? I haven't done this as much as you have."

"I told you I think she's very pretty," Bigelow said. "And I think she'll probably be willing, but—"

"I don't like the sound of that," Prudhomme said. "But what? Is she stupid? Lazy? Dishonest? Well, of course she's dishonest. All niggers are dishonest. What's your reservation?"

Bigelow pondered this for a moment. "I'm trying to think of a tactful way to put it," he said after a moment.

"Tactful? A tactful way to do what?" Prudhomme said fearfully. "What did you see?"

A frightening thought occurred to him. "It's her health, isn't it? What is it, typhus? Yellow fever?"

"No," Bigelow said slowly. "Least I don't think so. As I said before, it's a little early in the season for yellow fever. . . ." His voice trailed away as he looked off toward the other end of the building, where two men were feeling the knee joints of a boy who was perhaps ten years old.

"Then what?" Prudhomme said, almost shouting now: "Obviously you saw something. What was it?"

"Oh, it's probably nothing—my imagination, I suspect. This is an honest house, from all I hear."

"Let me be the judge of that," Prudhomme said. "I'm the one who's thinking of buying her. What is it you see?"

"You mean what do I think I see?"

"Yes, yes! What do you *think* you see?"

"Well," Bigelow said, drawing out his answer, "you see those two little red spots just above her upper lip? They're probably nothing, and even if they're what I suspect, you've probably been vaccinated, so you'd be perfectly fine."

"Smallpox!" Prudhomme breathed the word.

"Looks like it, a little bit," Bigelow said, nodding. "But as I said, it could be nothing at all. Just some sort of discoloration, like moles, or . . . something."

"But it's just two little spots!"

"True enough," Bigelow said. "That is, just two little spots *today*. This time tomorrow, there could be dozens, and when they start breaking open and oozing they'll be contagious—real contagious."

"What should I do, then?"

"Well, you could keep her in quarantine until you're certain," Bigelow said. "Keep her away from your other slaves until you know. Otherwise, the pox could sweep through the quarters and they'd die so fast you'd have to bury them two at a time and burn all their clothes."

"Oh, God."

"But that's only if it's the smallpox. And if it ain't, think about the fun you could have with this pretty little girl. Might be worth takin' the chance."

"Not *that big* a chance," Prudhomme said. "I got along without a fancy girl for years now. I ain't had the smallpox, myself, and I ain't planning to get it just so I can have a colored girl in my bed."

The man who called himself Nathan Bigelow watched as Prudhomme made his hasty retreat. The smile that crossed Bigelow's face remained only fleetingly before he strolled out of the market—in a direction, opposite to that taken by his companion. He walked north up Royale in a direction that was becoming familiar to him, finally entering the door of Pierre Dumond's wineshop. He was greeted there quietly by Josiah Beede.

"Any problems?" Beede asked, shutting the door behind them.

"Don't think so," the man who had been calling himself Bigelow said. "I got the feeling that Prudhomme—that's the man's name—ain't entirely sold on the idea himself. I think I managed to instill enough doubt in his mind, but I guess we won't know until he makes his move."

"Well, we can only hope," Beede said. "Randolph, especially, is uneasy about the situation. He's staked a lot on getting Louisa out of bondage."

"Well, I did what I could," the man said. "Guess now it's up to Prudhomme. I'd like to be around to see how it works out, but I gotta get back downriver. It'll be good to be Con Schneider again. Give my best to Randolph and tell him I'm pullin' for him."

"I shall."

"One other thing I meant to tell you," Schneider said. "I had a long talk the other day with George, Miz Hawkin's slave that's workin' for Howie. Turns out that he's the source of a lot of them gold half eagles I've been findin'. He had a little mold and he'd been makin' them now and then in the blacksmith's shop. And guess what he'd been usin' to make them from."

"British sovereigns," Beede said. "That'd be my guess."

"How did you . . . ?"

"As I said, it was a guess. But about thirty thousand dollars in British sovereigns disappeared from the British army just before the battle in 1815. Hawkins was in a Highland regiment that was nearly wiped out in that battle. Hawkins is likely the one who took them. Sovereigns would be about the right weight for converting to half eagles."

"You're right," Schneider said. "But George didn't get them from Hawkins. Howie found them, apparently, and started squirreling them away for his own use, and George somehow caught on to it. Howie stole them from Hawkins, and George stole them from Howie."

"So who do you suppose they belong to now?"

"Good question," Schneider said. "Queen Victoria, I suppose, but I don't think she's gonna get them back."

Chapter 33

Against his instincts, Nathaniel Prescott the Quaker cotton factor allowed himself to be persuaded to return to the slave market the following morning to attempt to buy the girl Louisa. He brought Beede with him so there would be a witness to his failure and to his good-faith attempt to consummate the purchase. As it happened, Prescott was the one who received the surprise.

"It's the girl you're interested in, if I'm not mistaken," said the dealer. "You're in luck, sir. My prospective purchaser has not returned, and I can't afford to keep feeding her. If you know of someone who's interested in buying a pretty young fancy, I feel certain we can work something out." He sent an assistant to the cells to retrieve the girl while the dealer called for coffee for his guests.

"Why did the purchaser not return?" Prescott asked. "You seemed quite certain when last I was here that she was spoken for."

"You're no more surprised than I am," the dealer said. "I was assured that the gentleman was a ready buyer, if the price were right. Perhaps he has suffered unforeseen financial reverses. I really can't say."

The assistant reappeared in the doorway with the girl in tow. He shoved the girl into the room and beat a hasty retreat. Prescott thought the behavior odd, but the dealer acted as if it were of no concern.

"She's a lovely little girl," the dealer said. "Turn around, missy, and let the man see you."

"I ain't feelin' too good," Louisa said. "I got a bad hurt in my stomach. I was shiverin' all last night, and I still don't feel right."

"Don't you give me none of your lip," the dealer said. "You stand up straight where the man can see you or I'll bend you double."

With apparent effort, the girl stood a bit straighter than before.

"You might have to take a whip to her a little bit," the dealer said. "Sometimes they get a little uppity when they're left alone for a while. They start gettin' bigheaded ideas and forgettin' their place."

"What're those red spots?" Prescott said.

"What red spots?"

"On her face, there," Prescott said. He pointed them out to the dealer. "Looks like she's got some on her arms, too."

"I don't know, sir," the dealer said as he backed away from the girl. "Nothing to be concerned about, I'm sure. She had no spots a couple of days ago."

"You mean they just appeared recently?" Prescott said in alarm. "They look suspiciously like . . ."

Beede had sat silently during this exchange, but now he spoke up.

"How much are you asking for her?"

The dealer studied his face as if he had not noticed his presence before.

"Well, sir," he said, "a fancy piece like this girl— she'll run you five hundred dollars minimum anywhere in town."

"Now, just a minute," Prescott said. "You can't sell this girl for—"

"Two-fifty," said Beede.

"I couldn't possibly go lower than four-fifty," the dealer said. "With what she's cost me in food . . . I gotta get something out of this."

"Three hundred," Beede said.

"Four hundred," the dealer said.

"No," said Beede. "Two-fifty."

Silence. Then, "Very well. Three hundred it is. I'm taking a terrible beating, sir, but sales are slow these days. I hope you're proud of yourself, taking advantage of an honest businessman like this."

"I am indeed," Beede said. He pulled three hundred-dollar notes from his pocket and handed them to the dealer, who studied them intently for a moment.

"I don't believe I know this bank," he said.

"The shavers will know it," Beede said. "It's a solid, solvent institution."

"They'll discount it, though," the dealer said. "For a bank in New Hampshire they'll probably deduct ten cents on the dollar. The fair thing for you to do would be to make up for my losses."

"If I walk out this door," Beede said, "you'll lose considerably more than ten percent."

The dealer considered this; then he delivered the bill of sale.

"All right, I've bought you. Will you come with me without making a scene?" Beede asked Louisa.

"Yessuh," she said. A trace of a smile played at the corners of her mouth.

"Then let's be off," Beede said, and he began walking rapidly toward Rue Royale.

Prescott held his tongue until they were a block away from the slave market. Then he lengthened his stride and pulled ahead of the little party, motioning to Beede to catch up with him.

"I didn't want to say anything to upset your negotiations," Prescott said. "Nevertheless, I wonder if you understand what you have done here."

"Certainly, sir. I purchased a slave. Although, strictly speaking, *I* did not buy her; I merely acted as Randolph's agent in the transaction, since he would not have been permitted to do so for himself."

"I followed that, Mr. Beede. But are you aware of the serious health threat this girl represents? The abdominal pains, the chills of which she complains, the red spots on her face and arms? These are the signs of smallpox in its early stages."

"Smallpox? Oh, I think not. She has not complained of aches or pains since we left the marketplace. I think it was only the tension of being displayed and inspected as if she were a tomato or a head of cabbage."

"But the red spots! Those are characteristic of the smallpox, and their presence indicates that she will soon be capable of spreading her infection to everyone she meets."

"Surely not," Beede said. "And unless I'm wrong I believe I can cure her."

"There is no cure, sir. One either lives or dies, and the outcome is beyond the control of man."

"Do you think so? Well, let us see."

Beede turned to Louisa, who still lagged a few paces behind the men. He motioned to her to join them.

"Louisa," he said when she had caught up, "Mr. Prescott is concerned about your health. Do you feel all right?"

"Oh, yessuh. I ain't felt better than this in years. I thanks you for that, sir."

"You can thank Randolph for that. We'll be seeing him in a few minutes. But no headaches, backaches? No chills or fever?"

"Oh, no, suh. I feels fine."

"You see, sir, she feels fine," Beede said to Prescott. "And as for these spots, they can be cleared up rather quickly."

Beede wet two fingers in his mouth, then placed them on Louisa's forehead and began rubbing. As Prescott watched in amazement, the first spot began to disappear, and he slowly began to comprehend.

"Well, I'll be damned," he said, forgetting his Quaker scruples about uttering oaths.

"See?" Beede said. "Why, in no time at all she'll be good as new."

"Berry juice? Some sort of rouge?"

"Cranberries," Beede said. "They're not often seen down here, but we have them in abundance in New England. Randolph brought them from New England; he is addicted to them."

Prescott shook his head. "If I were a gambler, I'd not like to face you across a card table," he said.

"I'm not a gambler, either," Beede said. "But I believe it's often helpful to study those who are."

They returned to Dumond's wineshop in a celebratory mood. Louisa was greeted by Randolph with open arms, and the couple shortly disappeared into another room. Dumond poured coffee—declaring that it was too early in the day for wine—and the small party relaxed in the courtyard to savor their victory.

"Now that you've retrieved Louisa, I guess you'll be wanting to get out of town pretty quick," Sheriff Schneider said at last.

"The thought had occurred to me," Beede said. "I believe we're out of danger momentarily, but there's no way to tell if trouble may arise again. Or when."

"I figured that," Schneider said. "I was sort of hoping, however, that you could assist me with this murder case I got before you fled the state."

"Esther Hawkins, you mean? I confess that in my concern for Randolph and Louisa, I had forgotten about the murder."

"Understandable," Schneider said. "But if you've got any ideas before you go, I'd sure be grateful for them."

"Do you have any suspects in mind now?" Beede asked.

"Well, Louisa. And this overseer, name of Travis. But I don't think Louisa done it, and Travis is nowhere to be found. I don't relish tryin' to track him down."

"Nobody closer to home?"

"You thinkin' of someone in particular?"

"Howie," Beede said. "Your deputy. He lives nearby. He knew Mrs. Hawkins and admits that he did odd jobs for her. And suddenly, you say, he has found a stash of gold coins."

"British sovereigns," Schneider said, as the possibilities dawned on him. "The slave George says that he got them out of a stash that Howie had hidden away. George thought Howie was going to use them to buy some slaves."

"Is this George fellow a blacksmith, also?" asked Prescott.

"Right," said Schneider. "About my height, with a complexion 'bout the color of old leather, with a tremendous chest."

"I'd be willing to bet that he was the one who's been supplying me with the money to buy and free slaves. He lives downriver a few miles on a cotton plantation?"

"That's the man," Schneider said.

They were disturbed by a knock on the door, an impatient but insistent rapping that resounded throughout the house. A moment later, Dumond's small young house slave appeared in the doorway of the room.

"Man at the door say he's wantin' M'sieur Beede," she said.

"Show him in, Clarissa," said Dumond.

The caller had not bothered to wait for the girl's return, for he appeared suddenly behind her in the doorway.

"I seek M'sieur Josiah Beede," he said to the room at large. "I'm told I could find him here."

"I'm Beede."

"M'sieur, I come on behalf of a man of this city

whom you know, M'sieur Achille Balfour. He has suffered insult at your hand and demands satisfaction. I bring a challenge from him. Do you accept the challenge?"

"Challenge?" Beede said, bewildered. "To a duel, you mean?"

"I do."

"What insult has he received? How did I defame him?"

"That is not my concern," the man said. "I am here merely to deliver this challenge and to receive your reply. Do you or do you not accept this challenge?"

"I believe I have not defamed or belittled M'sieur Balfour in any way," Beede said.

The visitor permitted himself a brief nod.

"Then I shall report to the gentleman that you have accepted the challenge and have agreed to meet him on the field of honor," he said. "I shall bid you gentlemen *adieu*. You shall hear from me again."

Chapter 34

"**You** cannot accept this challenge!" Randolph said in alarm the following day. "Balfour is an experienced duelist. His reputation is widespread. I heard of it even in my jail cell!"

"I assumed as much when he was so eager to challenge me. But it doesn't matter any longer. I have already accepted."

"In the name of God, why?" Randolph asked.

"My reputation is at stake," Beede said. "I have avoided dueling all my life, and I'm afraid it may already be too late to avoid a reputation for cowardice. But if I am ever to return to the South, I cannot appear to avoid this confrontation."

"You *can* apologize," Dumond pointed out. "Up until the time you are forced to take the field, it is permissible to make amends and avert disaster."

"Apologize for what? He says I accused him of counterfeiting, but I did not. I spoke the simple truth, and I didn't accuse him of anything. Moreover, I do not think my apology would be accepted. He intends to kill me, and this is his only legal opportunity to do so."

"I'm aware of that," Dumond said. "But truth, as you well know, is rarely a defense in matters of honor. It is perception that counts; the perception of honor is all."

"Then I am a dead man. I will not apologize for something I did not do nor, indeed, understand."

Randolph was thoughtful. "The other alternative," he said, "would be to win the duel."

"And how would I do that?" Beede asked bitterly. "By divine intervention? Do I will him to fire wildly into the trees?"

"I was thinking more along the lines of firing first and killing your opponent," Randolph said. "It's the traditional way to win a duel, I believe."

"And how can I hope to accomplish that?" Beede asked. "We are to meet at sunrise tomorrow at the Dueling Oak. I've not the time to become an experienced duelist in so short a time."

"It often happens," said Dumond, "that duels don't turn out as expected. Duels are unreliable things. Experience and skill often count for little when guns are selected. The flint may not spark, or the powder might not ignite. Pistols are smoothbore, so accuracy is less assured than with a rifle, and neither adversary is permitted to take aim. Take care to turn your side to him, so to present a smaller target, and fire the first shot. Shooting quickly is often more important than shooting accurately."

"I'll keep that in mind," Beede said doubtfully.

"I can attest to the value of shooting quickly," said Schneider. "I've seen it with my own eyes."

"If we had more time we could engage the services of someone with experience, to train you in the art of dueling. But we haven't the time, and I don't suppose you could prevail on Balfour to postpone the meeting for a day or two in order to prepare you properly."

"I would not ask, even if I thought I might succeed," Beede said. "The fear of humiliation weighs on me more heavily than the thought of death."

He felt differently in the morning, however.

Chapter 35

He had always known that it would end like this.

Lying in his bed in New Hampshire, far from the land where men faced each other with loaded pistols at the crack of dawn, he could console himself by imagining his conduct in such an event. In his dreams, he was always courageous, standing without flinching as the bullet hurtled toward him from the barrel of his adversary's weapon, growing larger and larger in his field of vision. And always, in his dreams, he survived to return home, where Adrienne would be waiting fearfully for that knock on the door that—because he had survived—would never come. There would be rejoicing, then, and tenderness, and that would make his brush with death worthwhile.

Strange that he never imagined the fate of his opponent. His adversaries in dream were faceless men. No matter how hard he tried, he could not identify them, and they disappeared from his dreams as soon as the shots were fired.

But his dreams were not realistic, and he well knew it. In his waking hours he would admit to himself that he would not be such a hero in life. He knew how firmly cowardice ruled his soul.

And now, standing under the great oaks two days later on a plantation a few miles from the city and awaiting Balfour's arrival, he feared that his timidity was likely to win out over whatever residue of courage he might possess. In the chill morning half-light he shivered uncontrollably, not entirely due to the cold.

I will be shaking too violently to get a proper aim, he thought. As a practical matter, he was unlikely to have the time to aim, which was not permitted in any event. The object of dueling was to bring the gun to bear quickly, in a single fluid motion, and fire quickly, trusting that the weapon's balance would bring it to the proper position. Pausing to aim was, in a sense, an admission of cowardice.

So he would not aim, but he had no doubts that his cowardice would, nevertheless, find him out.

In less than an hour, he would be dead.

"A carriage is coming," Dumond said.

Two carriages, actually, Beede saw. One would be carrying Balfour and his second. The other, a hearse, would carry Beede's corpse back to the city after Balfour had finished with him. Beede recognized the mental game for what it was—Balfour's attempt at intimidation—but recognition did not diminish its effectiveness.

He did not want to die. Undoubtedly, neither did

Balfour, but he did not seem concerned about that eventuality. He must have had more confidence in his own marksmanship than Beede, who had none.

The two carriages pulled up alongside, and Balfour and his second descended. Dumond excused himself to Beede and joined Balfour's second at some remove from the dueling parties. A third man now left the carriage and moved to one side: the physician who would be called on to tend the wounded or to issue the declaration of death.

His death!

Beede hated himself for his fears. He looked with distaste at his trembling hands, mortified at the convulsion in his belly. He attempted to reason himself out of—if not his own cowardice—at least this shameful public display of it. Balfour must not know of it.

But a quick glance told him that Balfour knew already. He doffed his scruffy top hat in Beede's direction and favored him with a smile that was smug and condescending. Beede felt his face grow hot, and he turned away with a sense of shame.

"Shall we begin?" said Balfour's second. "It grows late."

Beede walked through his paces as if in a dream, a particularly macabre nightmare from which he, in all likelihood, would never awaken. The two men took their positions barely ten paces apart, pistols ready, pointed to the sky, and awaited instructions.

Already, Beede could feel himself shaking. He glanced at his gun and despaired of ever holding it steady enough to fire it accurately. He stared at the barrel, willing himself to hold it steady. The sun caught his eyes and tickled his nose.

"Are you ready, gentlemen?" A wave of fear passed over him, and he knew himself irrevocably a coward. A cold sweat had broken out on his face. His gun was waving wildly. Perhaps the others could not see it, but it was all too clear to him. The sun was bothering him If he were forced to sneeze, he would certainly fire wild.

"You may fire at will."

He brought his gun to bear, or attempted to, and saw Balfour doing the same. As Beede began to squeeze the trigger, the sneeze overcame him. It racked his body and caused him to double over in a convulsion.

And in that moment, Balfour fired his weapon.

Beede heard the ball whistle over his head and felt the passing breeze.

A shocked silence pervaded.

"Dishonorable!" shouted Balfour. "Coward!"

"You have not yet fired your weapon," Dumond said to Beede. "M'sieur Balfour has had his shot at you. Now he must receive yours."

"I have no desire to shoot. I hold no grudge against this man."

"Coward!" shouted Balfour. "Coward! Coward! Coward!"

"He sneezed," Dumond said in reply. "He was facing into the sun, and it caused him to sneeze. I doubt not that the choice of direction was your doing. You cannot cry foul if your plotting works against you."

Beede looked at Dumond in surprise.

"Go ahead and shoot," Dumond said. "This cannot end until you return fire."

Beede shook his head. "I didn't want this duel.

M'sieur Balfour has had his chance at me. Let there be an end to it now."

He laid the gun on the grass and walked away with Balfour's angry screams echoing in his ears. He steeled himself not to turn and look back, even at the sounds of an urgent scuffle. He continued walking away, not so fast that he would appear to be fleeing, and he hardly noticed the sound of a second shot until a bullet whistled past his ear and lodged itself at head height in an ancient hickory tree a few yards ahead.

He turned around at that and saw Balfour lying pinned on the ground by his own second.

"He attempted to use your weapon to shoot you as you walked away," Dumond said, approaching. "I suppose he was so enraged at the outcome that he decided to take matters into his own hands."

"I'm grateful to you for preventing it."

"I did nothing to prevent it," Dumond said. "I would have done so, certainly, if I had realized what he was up to, but I didn't comprehend. I had forgotten about the loaded pistol that you had left lying on the ground. It was M'sieur Balfour's own second who prevented the attempt on your life."

"I suppose I should be grateful to him for saving my life."

"Indeed you should," Dumond said, "although I suspect he acted less to save your life than to salvage M'sieur Balfour's reputation."

Beede stopped walking. A question had suddenly arisen in his mind, and he paused to give it his full attention.

"But why?" he said.

"Pardon?"

"I'm attempting to understand why Balfour took offense at my simple statement that he seemed to be on good terms with Devall," Beede said. "It is only to be expected that they would be acquainted with each other if Devall is Madame Hawkins's nephew, as he claims to be. Balfour has admitted that he is the one who purchased Louisa for Madame Hawkins. Clearly the seeds of a relationship would be apparent to anyone who knew them."

"Devall says he has been living in Arkansas for the past few years," Dumond pointed out. "If he speaks the truth, his acquaintance with Balfour might not be quite so obvious."

"Perhaps so," Beede said. "But why should Balfour take offense if the acquaintance were made public? Surely an innocent and aboveboard relationship is nothing to be concerned about."

"Unless, of course, it *isn't* innocent," Dumond said. "Or aboveboard. You might do well to devote some thought to that."

Beede gave some thought to that possibility as he returned to New Orleans. By the time he arrived, a number of possibilities, none of them pleasant, had occurred to him.

Chapter 36

Howie Boudreau returned home two days after Louisa's liberation. He groomed and stabled his horse and walked back to the house. The door, which he had been careful to lock on his departure, now stood open. He fought down a sudden sense of panic; there was, after all, no particular reason for concern.

Conrad Schneider was in the parlor, warming himself by a newly built fire.

"Evenin,' Sheriff," Howie said. "How'd you get in here?"

"It wasn't hard," Schneider said. "I picked the lock with a knife; took about a minute. You should really get better locks."

"I'll keep it in mind," Howie said. "What're you doin'?"

"Just waitin' for you to get back. Where've you been?"

"Oh, just up to Red River country," Howie said. "Up to Buffalo Bayou."

"Visitin'?"

"That's right." And looking for land, he said to himself, but not to Schneider. Howie thought he would be needing quite a lot of land, and ideally it would be land that was far away from here.

"Find what you were lookin' for?" Schneider said, as if he could read minds.

"Could be," Howie said. "Could well be."

"I've been lookin' for somethin' myself," Schneider said. "And I found it."

"What's that?" Howie wasn't really interested, but it was good business to keep your employer happy, and Schneider, for the time being, was still his employer.

"I found this," Schneider said, and fished the dueling pistol from the pocket of his coat. "Unless I miss my guess, it's the gun that killed old Esther Hawkins. And I found it in your house. I'm going to have to arrest you for her murder. Probably for the murder of the overseer, too."

"No! It ain't fair! It was a accident! I didn't mean to kill her!"

"And I guess you didn't mean to run away and take the murder weapon with you, neither."

"I . . . I wasn't thinkin' right," Howie said. "It was a mistake. I'm sorry about it now."

"Why'd you kill the old lady, Howie?" Schneider said. "She never did you no harm."

"I came to see her about buyin' those duelin' pistols," Howie said. "She never used them, and I was goin' to need them after I became a gentleman. So she let me load them and try them out. One of them just went off. I thought the ball must be buried in the wall somewhere, but I guess it hit her. She stared at me for a second, like I'd broke wind or spit on her floor, and she collapsed right there in front of me."

"Why didn't you go for help?"

"What kind of help?" Howie said. "She was dead, Sheriff! Weren't nothin' I could do for her. Scared me so much that I lit out with the pistol in my hand, not thinkin' about the one I left behind. I've been lookin' for a way to get it back ever since."

"How were you goin' to become a gentleman, Howie?" Schneider said. "You're a blacksmith. Blacksmiths don't get to be gentlemen."

"I weren't goin' to be a blacksmith much longer. Miz Hawkins had promised to give me a couple of slaves. I planned to let George run the blacksmith business, and I would take it easy. I thought I'd put that Louisa to work in the kitchen—and maybe some other places, too."

"So what happened?"

"I waited for nearly a year, even waited until after the harvest was done, and when I come back to see her buy the guns, I asked about the slaves. She said she'd changed her mind. She said she'd decided to free them all! Said she couldn't bear to keep on livin' as a slaveholder. It was morally wrong, she said."

"There's others that feel that way, too," Schneider pointed out.

"Yeah? Well, she didn't feel that way before! She's had slaves ever since she came to Louisiana, and she didn't complain none until just recent, when I tried to hold her to her promise! Now, suddenly, she gets scruples! Don't that sound suspicious to you?"

"Suspicious? How so?"

"Well, look at it, Sheriff. Just look at it. I'm trash, is how she sees it! I don't *deserve* to have slaves! Well, damn it to hell, I'm as good as the next man, and better'n some I could name. I deserve to have slaves as much as anybody, I do. And she knew it, too. She didn't like me much, but she knew I was as deservin' as anybody."

"I don't think this was about you, Howie," Schneider said. "Miz Hawkins told Louisa she was going to free her, the day before you killed her."

"That's what Louisa says," Howie said, with a brief, bitter laugh. "Well, hell, what do you expect? She's a slave!"

"You think she's lyin'?"

"Well, sure she's lyin'. She's a slave! That's what they do! They try to talk their way out of things! You can't trust a slave to tell the truth; anybody from the South could tell you that."

"On the other hand," Schneider said, "it jibes with what you just told me yourself."

Howie ignored Beede as if he had never spoken. "Look at it for yourself, Sheriff. Miz Hawkins had a couple of thousand dollars' worth of slaves here. It don't make sense that she would just give 'em up like that. It's too big an investment."

"If that's true," Schneider said, "why'd you think she'd give 'em to you?"

"I didn't want 'em all! Just a couple: Louisa and that George that I got workin' in the blacksmith shop. That's all I needed. It wouldna hurt her to give up just two. But no, I weren't good enough."

"She decided not to give them away, Howie. That was her right."

"No, it wasn't," Howie said, the bitterness dripping from his voice. "She had no right at all. It was just to keep me down."

Schneider let Howie sulk for a while. When the deputy had calmed down a bit, Schneider decided to change the subject.

"How'd you know about the money?" Schneider asked.

"Ol' man Hawkins was a bragger," Howie said. "He was always hintin' that he had this stash of money. He used to say, kind of roundabout, you know, that he'd come into some money in Scotland and brung it with him to New Orleans. He kept sayin' that he had to change it some so nobody'd know where it come from. He must of stole it, I guess. He never said."

"But you didn't believe him?"

"Look at the way he lived. If he was loaded, like he said, why didn't he fix up that house of his? Ol' lady Hawkins coulda had three or four more house servants instead of just Louisa."

"But at some point you changed your mind?" Beede asked.

"After he died, I started comin' around more, helpin' Miz Hawkins, runnin' errands and such. I felt sorry for her some, I guess. And I thought she liked me some. She was always happy to see me."

"How'd you find the money?" Schneider asked.

"It was mostly accidental-like," Howie said. "Hawkins had buried it under the house. It was pretty

easy to find because it had been dug up recent, and I
could see the fresh dirt. I dug it up again, and there was
this strongbox full of gold sovereigns and a mold for
turnin' them into half eagles."

"So you took them for yourself."

"Well, hell, Sheriff! Hawkins was dead. Miz
Hawkins didn't need that kind of money. Travis had
found it and had used the mold to make a couple of
coins for hisself. I deserved them more than he did. But
he came back while I was stuffin' my saddlebags, so I
didn't have no choice. He tried to bargain with me like
I was just a thief, like him. After I shot him, I threw him
over my saddle and walked down to the river. They've
probably found him down around Pilot Town by now—
whatever's left of him that the 'gators didn't want."

"Howie, I gotta take you in. You know that."

"It ain't fair," Howie said. "I worked hard all my life.
I've had to kowtow to these Creole gentlemen and their
uppity wives all these years. All I wanted was a couple
of slaves to ease my burden."

"So what do you think of his story?" Schneider
asked when he met Beede in New Orleans two
days later. "About the money, I mean. Sounds a little
fishy to me."

"I suspect it's true enough, as far as it goes," Beede
said. "I don't think he knows the whole truth, though. I
don't think Hawkins *told* him the whole truth."

"About what?"

"About where the money came from. I think it's unlikely that Hawkins brought the money from England.
He was an enlisted man in a Highland regiment. How

would he carry several thousand dollars in gold coins in his kit? Beyond that, how would he hide them aboard ship, in close quarters? It would be a difficult feat for an officer; it would be impossible for a man in the ranks. I think he came by his money in America."

"They *were* British coins, though. Are you thinkin' he stole a payroll?"

"No. Too much gold. Only the highest-ranking officers would have been highly paid enough to warrant payment in gold. The entire British army in America would not have accounted for a full strongbox."

"Well, if the money didn't come from the army, where did he get it? Robbin' an American bank sure wouldn't of done it."

"No, that's true enough," Beede said. "I think it came from the army, all right. The British brought it across the ocean with them, but not to pay their troops."

"Then why?"

"Jean Lafitte," Beede said. "The gossip is that they brought about thirty thousand dollars in gold sovereigns to America in the hope that they could turn Lafitte to their side. They also offered him a commission in the Royal Navy."

"And he turned it down?"

"Yes. He put them off for a few days while he negotiated with the Americans, and in the end he turned the British down. After that, the British were preoccupied for a while with the coming battle, and after the battle— with most of their officers dead or wounded—the money seemed to lose its importance for a while."

Schneider shook his head. "I don't know," he said. "The British always keep a close watch on their money.

If that much gold disappeared, they'd a come lookin' for it."

"They did, I suspect, but by that time several weeks had passed, and too many men had died or deserted. Representatives of His Majesty's government were none too popular in these regions in those days, and I don't think many local people would be inclined to help them. I suspect the British simply couldn't find it."

"But old man Hawkins knew how to find it, you think?"

"My guess is that he's the one who stole it and buried it in the first place. Then he simply waited for the smoke to clear, dug it up, and moved it to his property."

"Makes sense, I guess," Schneider said. "You think some of it's still out there?"

"Probably a little of it. It was a lot of money."

"Think we can find it?"

"Not unless Howie tells us," Beede said. "He's probably the only one who knows."

"Well," Schneider said, "I ain't gonna lose much sleep over it. If I found it, I'd probably just have to turn it over to someone else, anyway. There ain't much incentive in that."

Chapter 37

"I ain't never slept in a bed before," Louisa said. "Just a pallet on the kitchen floor, mostly. I 'spect I could get used to this." She favored Randolph with a luxurious stretch intended to display her physical charms.

"No reason why you can't get used to it," Randolph said indulgently. "I have a bed at home, on my farm. It's a gift from the man who willed me the farm. As my wife, I permit you—expect you—to share it with me."

She stiffened, turned to face him. Outside, the churning of the riverboat's sternwheel set up a rhythmic counterpoint to their discussion.

"I'll share your bed for now, but I ain't your wife. You know we ain't married."

"Sure we are. Don't you remember?"

"Jumpin' a broom ain't marryin'," she said. "You know that well as I do."

"You want a ceremony? In a church with a preacher? I can probably arrange that, too."

"That ain't what I mean! You knows better'n that. Ain't no words gonna make me married to you, or you to me. When we did that little jumpin'-the-broom thing we was both slaves. Didn't matter what we said, 'cause we didn't really have no choices. Now you're free, and I'm free. We got choices now."

"You sayin' you don't want to be married to me?"

"I don't mean that, either," she said. "Fact is, nuther of us know what we wants just yet. We got to think on it."

"I've thought about it."

"It dint mean anythin' then because we didn't have no choices."

"So now you have choices," Randolph said. "You're free."

"I know. And that means I got to live with my choices. And I don't plan on makin' *any* choices without thinkin' on them. We ain't seen each other, hardly, for near five years. There's a lot I don't know about you. There's a lot you don't know about me."

"That's not true," Randolph said. "Not about me, at least. I know you like the back of my hand."

Louisa turned to look at him.

"Did you know I'se pregnant?"

His silence gave her the answer.

"What I figgered," she said. "I'se showin' more every day, but you never noticed. That overseer, that Travis, was havin' me every night just about. Weren't nothin' I could do about it. I figger I'se about five months along now. 'Long about August I'll be havin' a baby. How you feel about bein' a father to some other man's baby? A *white* man's baby?"

Silence. Then, "Did you love him?"

"I didn't even *like* him very much!" she said heatedly. "But I was a slave, and he was a overseer, and you . . . where was *you* long about last November? You sure wasn't by my side, pullin' that man off of me."

"I was in Alexandria," he said quietly. "I was at the house where you used to live. I was looking for you. It's taken me this long to find you and set you free."

She began to cry, and he found himself crying with her. They held each other, rocking quietly on the bed.

"I know, honey," she said. "And I *is* grateful to you for all you done. And if grateful was enough, I'd go through that marryin' ceremony right here and now. But you know it ain't enough, same as I do."

He had to admit to himself that she was right. This was a new life for both of them, and there would be many trials ahead, and they would have to weather at least a few of them before they could be sure of their future together. There would be hardship, and hard work, and thousands of adjustments to make before they could claim to be married, not least of which was a child—a mulatto child—who was not his progeny but would, nevertheless, be his responsibility.

"I'll do what you want me to do," he said finally. "Whatever it is. Even if you want to go back south and be a slave again, I'll get you back safely, somehow. You just have to tell me."

"What I want is to be with you," she said. "I just have to find out if I can. If you can give me some time, I'll try to make it as easy on you as I know how. Is that all right with you?"

He thought a moment but said nothing. Instead, he took her in his arms again and held her close.

On deck, Beede and Tomkins stood in companionable silence at the railing, watching the riverbank pass slowly by.

"How did you know that we were in need of assistance?" Beede asked finally. "I didn't know, myself, until a few days ago."

"Your friend Mr. Dumond knew," Israel Tomkins said. "I suppose he had a sense that matters were not progressing well. Judging from what I saw in that courtroom, I suspect that such matters *rarely* progress well. I understand that able-bodied men and attractive young women are in considerable demand, and the temptation to acquire them—by any means possible—must be substantial."

"You understand correctly," Beede said. "Nevertheless, I believed that the court would have taken my assertions at face value, particularly in light of the preposterous claims of our adversaries. I was naive, I fear."

"Well, my Deborah did not so believe," Tomkins said. "And in any event, she insisted that we should not gamble. She believed that time was of the essence. I would have been content to bundle the appropriate papers and send them to you by post, but Deborah wouldn't hear of it. She insisted—rightly, as it turns out—that my personal testimony might be required. I strongly suspect, although she did not say so, that she feared that you might again be seduced by New Orleans and choose not to return to your farm."

"There's little danger of that," Beede said.

"Nevertheless, I believe it concerned her. Incidentally, I should not be telling you such things, and I shall deny it if you mention it in her presence."

"I'm grateful to you for your timely intervention," he said to Tomkins. "But I wonder that you undertook such a journey on the strength of an assertion of a girl so young."

"Deborah is not merely a young girl, as you put it," Tomkins said. "She is my eldest daughter. Her mother and I have raised her to be resourceful and self-reliant, and she has proved to be all of that. Indeed, if I had not elected to come to New Orleans, I might have awakened some morning to find that she had decided to make the journey on her own. It was all I could do to persuade her not to accompany me."

"She is a headstrong girl, then."

"Yes, I suppose so," Tomkins said. "Headstrong is, of course, one of those names under which self-assurance often masquerades. Its carnival dress, if you will."

It was the second week in March, and the world on the riverbank—never truly bare, even in midwinter—was already bathed in a glow of green. At home in New England, Beede knew, snow would lie all around him, and the nights would still be frigid and dark. But here, in the swampy jungles of Louisiana, magnolia trees were preparing to bloom.

"You must have traveled with the speed of lightning," Beede said. "When Randolph and I came to New Orleans, the trip took the better part of three weeks."

"That is because you came by sailing ship," Tomkins pointed out. "I came by steamboat, and it made all the difference. It's a much more direct route by river. If I hadn't made the journey myself, I would never have believed we could journey from New England to New Orleans in such a short time."

"I'm grateful to you, but I'm surprised as well. This journey cannot have been inexpensive. I am astonished that you chose to undertake it merely because your daughter suggested it."

Tomkins stopped in his tracks and turned to face Beede directly.

"Mr. Beede, there are two things you must know about my daughter," he said, jabbing his pudgy finger in Beede's chest for emphasis. "And the first is that it is foolish to ignore Deborah's suggestions, for she is almost always in the right."

"And the second?"

"Ah, the second." Tomkins smiled sweetly. "Well, sir, the second is that this was not a suggestion; it was a direct order. I did not feel that I had the right to refuse."

"You *are* her father," Beede said.

"Yes," Tomkins said. "I am. And someday, when you are older and wiser—and married to my daughter—you will understand the limitations of such a position."

"I had not decided whether to ask her hand in marriage," Beede said.

"I'm aware of that."

"Or that she would have me."

Tomkins nodded, still wearing the beatific smile. "And are you under the impression," he said, "that it is your decision to make?"

Beede opened his mouth, but no words came out. Seeing this, Tomkins nodded as if he had received confirmation of a sort. His smile grew wider still, and Beede had the impression that, for a moment, the older man's ears disappeared entirely.

"Yes, I thought so," Tomkins said. "Well, it will be interesting to discover the truth, will it not?"

Belowdecks, a bell was ringing.

"I believe that's the call to breakfast," Tomkins said. "Shall we go below?"

"I should arrange to have a meal delivered to Randolph and Louisa," Beede said. "No doubt they'll be hungry after their ordeal."

"No doubt," said Tomkins. "But it's been my experience that newly wedded couples—which, in a sense, they are—often can take their minds off their stomachs for extended periods of time. Let's not disturb them just now."

Beede thought of his farm awaiting him in Warrensboro, and he thought of Deborah Tomkins, who was also waiting—apparently with great eagerness—for his return. And he thought of Randolph, finally reunited with the woman he bought out from slavery, the two of them sleeping peacefully in the stateroom below.

"I remain curious, however, about another matter," Tomkins said after a bit. "Perhaps there's no answer, but it *is* curious."

"And what is that?"

"It's about the duel with M'sieur Balfour," Tomkins said. "I know little of dueling, but it seems to me—from what you and Pierre have said—that by sneezing when you did, and then walking away without firing a shot, you robbed your adversary of whatever satisfaction he might have achieved on the field of honor."

"Yes," Beede said. "I believe I did. He was, to say the least, put out about it."

"Which leads me to my question: Why did he not

simply challenge you again? Surely he was not prepared to drop the issue entirely."

"No, not at first," Beede said. "I wondered about that
myself, but Con Schneider had looked into Balfour's
background and explained the situation to Randolph
and me yesterday morning."

"Is that what caused the three of you to break into
laughter on the quay? I assumed he was telling you a
humorous story."

"He was, in a manner of speaking," said Beede,
"though I doubt that Balfour found it so amusing."

"What was it, then, or is it something you are not
permitted to tell?"

"Oh, I think I can tell you," Beede said. "It seems
that Balfour didn't dare challenge me again because
Sheriff Schneider, and perhaps others, had learned his
secret. Con had spent some time looking into property
records and had found that Balfour was descended from
a hired man at a nearby plantation and his common-law
wife."

"And this had some special meaning?"

"It meant that his mother was a Negro. It meant that
Balfour would himself be considered a colored man
passing for white. Men of color are not permitted to
duel; they're not 'honorable' enough. Sheriff Schneider
said he had sent a message to Balfour at the mint, informing him of his findings, the day before the duel. I
suppose Balfour thought he could get away with it if he
killed me before the word got out. When I survived, he
was in grave danger."

"Balfour is colored? I find that difficult to believe.
Why, he's as white as you or me."

"In Louisiana," Beede said, "a man is considered to

be a Negro if he has as little as one thirty-second part Negro blood. And Balfour—if Con's figuring is correct—has quite a bit more than that."

"Astonishing," said Tomkins.

"Many aspects of the slave system are astonishing," Beede said. "A man can be white one moment and colored the next. It takes no more than a rumor to ruin a man's life forever. Normally, I would not support an effort to 'out' a man on such grounds, but in this case I'm not so bothered by it, particularly if it means he will leave us alone."

"And Devall? Is he also a 'man of color,' as they say here?"

"That may very well prove to be the case," Beede said. "M'sieur Devall seems to have disappeared entirely. If he is colored and attempting to pass for white, he could be in for a great deal of trouble. If he is ever found—and I'd wager that he won't be—the law will go very hard on him."

"I have never heard such absurdity," Tomkins said. "And the greatest absurdity is that I believe every word."

"I know," Beede said. "All too strange, yet all too true." He leaned on the deck railing and watched the river pass by at their feet. Not so long ago, he thought, to sail upstream on the Mississippi River was considered futile at best. Fur traders would drift down the river on their cobbled-together flatboats, but they would sell them for lumber in New Orleans and walk back home. And yet, here they were, sailing upstream—laboriously, true, but unmistakably—under the power of steam.

Perhaps the Unitarians were right after all. Perhaps man was perfectible, despite his quite evident faults, and he needed only to perfect his environment before he could turn his attention to improving himself. Beede would not have thought so, even a day before, but then he would not have thought it possible to make headway upstream against the Mississippi, either.

Well, he thought, we shall see.

They were approaching a bend in the river, and the boat's whistle released a loud, harmonious blast that shook the leaf buds on the embankment. The sound echoed faintly back to him, and it seemed to Beede that it sounded particularly musical this morning.

Afterword

In her chronicle of her life after Little Rock Central High School, *White Is a State of Mind*, Melba Patillo Beals, one of the original "Little Rock Nine," explained why she did not return to the school for her senior year: during the summer her mother received a call from a close relative in Georgia, who informed her that diehard racists there were planning to come to Arkansas and assassinate the young desegregation pioneer. Based on this information, her family chose to send Melba to school in California, a measure that might well have saved her life.

This information was taken seriously in part because of the source. Her relative, who was light-skinned, had managed to pass for white and had been elected county sheriff. For protective coloration, he also had joined the local Ku Klux Klan, and it was through his Klan associates that he learned of the planned assassination.

The incident offers further evidence, if any were needed, that racial distinctions in the South were not only arbitrary and capricious but also, frequently, highly fanciful.

To give substance to these dubious distinctions, Southerners devised a spectrum of narrow, not to say hairsplitting, categories of color distinctions, many with their own distinctive names, and assigned economic values to each. As a general rule, lighter skin brought higher prices, and light-skin servants were more likely to be assigned to domestic duties rather than to field work.

Vestiges of this attitude remain today, although they seem to be fading. (There was a day when hospitals routinely separated "white" blood from "Negro" blood to prevent inadvertent mixing during transfusions.) It is only one of many aspects of the southern experience tinged with a touch of comedy along with the tragedy.

Historical novelists depend on the advice and expertise of others. In my case, the "others" are legion. In particular, Pamela Arcenaux and her staff at the Historic New Orleans Collection, and Greg Lambousy at the Old United States Mint in New Orleans, now part of the Louisiana State Museum, were extremely helpful. I'm grateful also to the staffs of the New Orleans Metropolitan Convention and Visitors' Bureau and the Holiday Inn Downtown Superdome. Especially I'd like to thank Jeff McClurken, assistant professor of history at Mary Washington College, who read the manuscript and made a number of valuable suggestions.

In New Hampshire, 1836, Josiah Beede's
quiet life is about to change forever...

Death of a Mill Girl

0-425-18713-6

By

Clyde Linsley

"Linsley writes with a sparse elegance
reminiscent of Dick Francis."
—*Under the Covers*

*It is the autumn of 1836, and the body of a
beautiful young woman has been discovered on
the farm of retired lawyer and military hero
Josiah Beede. Now, Josiah must lure a killer
out of hiding before another innocent
is murdered—or the wrong suspect is hanged.*

"Linsley weaves the finest threads of the historical
mystery...into an irresistable tapestry."
—Ann McMillan

MIRIAM GRACE MONFREDO

brings to life one of the most exciting periods in our nation's history—the mid-1800s—when the passionate struggles of suffragettes, abolitionists, and soldiers touched the lives of every American, including a small-town librarian named Glynis Tryon...

SENECA FALLS INHERITANCE	0-425-14465-8
NORTH STAR CONSPIRACY	0-425-14720-7
BLACKWATER SPIRITS	0-425-15266-9
THROUGH A GOLD EAGLE	0-425-15898-5
THE STALKING HORSE	0-425-16695-3
MUST THE MAIDEN DIE	0-425-17610-X

The Seneca Falls series continues into the Civil War with Glynis's niece Bronwen Llyr, who goes undercover and behind enemy lines in the service of Pinkerton's Detective Agency.

SISTERS OF CAIN	0-425-18092-1
BROTHERS OF CAIN	0-425-18638-5
CHILDREN OF CAIN	0-425-19130-3

LOVE MYSTERY?

From cozy mysteries to procedurals,
we've got it all. Satisfy your cravings with our monthly
newsletters designed and edited specifically for fans of who-
dunits. With two newsletters to choose from, you'll be sure to
get it all. Be sure to check back each month or sign up for
free monthly in-box delivery at

www.penguin.com

Berkley Prime Crime

Berkley publishes the premier writers of mysteries.
Get the latest on your
favorties:
Susan Wittig Albert, Margaret Coel, Earlene
Fowler, Randy Wayne White, Simon Brett, and
many more fresh faces.

Signet

From the Grand Dame of mystery,
Agatha Christie, to debut authors,
Signet mysteries offer something for every reader.

*Sign up and sleep with
one eye open!*